Julian Thomas

———

Tales Gathered by the Wayside

———

Also by Julian Thomas:
Zita
The Delicate Magic of Life
Walk With Me, Always
Namesake and Other Stories
The Bridge
Just Us
Oh! Betsan, Theres Lovely You Are
Gaffer and Co
The Pinnacle

Contents

The House at Number Seven

There was no hint the day would be any different from yesterday. Or the day before that, or even the day when rain last fell. The sun shone shortening shadows as midday advanced. Dust lay forgotten in the gutters. Air, weighted by heat, sapped strength from the living. The dead were gone. The curtains drawn. The streets deserted. At Number Seven a plastic fan perched on an upright piano tossed warm air in a desultory manner uncertain if it was worth the bother. A table, centred and once polished to a shine, had a layer of dust into which a heart had been drawn. Initials *A* and *B* were inscribed on each side. The town clock echoed. The long afternoon stretched.

Albert stood by the piano, his mind swiped clean by uncertainty. He blasphemed to himself, to Betty and to all the nobodies who were not there. 'God, look at me now! I can't even read the lyrics without bloody weeping!' He wanted to see the lyrics, though he knew the words. The sheet music stared back at him, washed over by tears and unfocused. He lacked the emotional strength to read or sing them as once he did. He sensed Betty was looking down, eyeing him, urging him, he never being a faint-hearted man in all the years they had been man and wife. He thought if she did not make heaven no one would! Now he was bust. A lonely man. The dust of life dragging him down. 'God help me,' he blasphemed again. He wiped away a tear with the back of his hand, snatched at the music that had been there like an icon since Betty had passed away, and reversed it roughly—shut its eyes, closed down its sound, Betty's sound, the sound of her playing, her music. 'I can't do it. Dear God, I can't do it!' He paced around the table, glanced as a miscreant might at the sight of his own mischief, at the blinded and dumbed sheet music from whom he had wilfully removed sight and sound. 'Dear God, why did she leave me? And leave that music? There! That song of all songs! My Betty, who was so tidy, a so putting-things-away sort of a person. Neat. Trim. Self and house. Just left it there like a bloody sentry in a sentry box. To remind me? Of all the music she could have left … this one, this very one, this lasting message.' He began, slowly, to hum its melody. He tried his voice, a brush of guilt rising up when no guilt existed. He drew in the words, began. 'Love me tender, love me true, never let me go …'

There was a gentle tap on the front window. He wasn't sure. He stopped singing, and listened. Another gentle tap. Yes, there it was again! He went into the hall. Tiled. Victorian, gloomy. The front door panelled with frosted glass. He could see a distorted outline of a woman on the other side.

'Good God, who the fuck can that be? Some well-heeled, middle-class do-gooder. Jesus! Now they call!' he mumbled. Upset, and wasted he shouted at the door.

'I'm dead. You're too fucking late!'

The distortion vanished, dropped below the door's

wooden panel.

Gone.

As Albert turned to go back the letterbox was pushed open and two eyes appeared like a fox in the night. Red-rimmed with dust, and tired. The eyes of a waif, and letterbox high.

'Albert, it's me. Doreen. Betty's friend.'

'Doreen? Oh! ... the Doreen who lives by the railway station?'

'Yes.'

'Good God, woman, you shouldn't be out mid afternoon! You shouldn't be out at all. What do you want?'

'Come to see you're okay.'

'I'm probably dead. Just trying to sing so I know I'm not.'

'Can I come in?'

'Haven't got much to offer you.' He opened the door and Doreen, not expecting the speed with which Albert moved, nearly fell across the threshold. 'You're done-in dear. Let me help you.' He took her elbow. 'Dear God, you're all bone. You not eating? Or you're sick. Whichever, it's not good. Come in. I've got bottled water. Guaranteed free from sand and sewage. Look at the state of you. Just you sit in Betty's chair and I'll get the water. Drink from the bottle. Don't waste a drop if we do that.' Albert disappeared into the kitchen. 'Dear God, it's the fucking plague. You want a bit of bread and cheese, Doreen,' he called out. No reply. He came back in with the water. Doreen was slumped, eyes closed. He stared hard. 'Don't you go dying on me! What will the neighbours say!' He put down the bottle of water

3

and gently prodded her shoulder with his index finger. 'You okay?' She didn't move. He gave her a more determined prod. The weight of the dead was light: skin and bone. Fleshless. He felt her pulse. Wrist. Neck. 'Dearest Betty, forgive me. I shouldn't be touching her. You just gone, and she just arrived! Look for yourself. Her eyelids are down. Were my fingers insensitive to you? I can't feel a pulse.' He had another go. Nothing. He did what he had seen doctors do on television: lifted an eyelid. 'Dear God, what am I looking for? A spark. A blink. A fucking wink! She couldn't have died that quick. Lively as a rabbit the other side of the door.' He opened the bottle of water and shoved his finger down the top, and gently massaged her lips with his damp finger. 'I'm not going to wake the dead this way! Hey, Doreen, your lips are bad. All cracked and dry. Should have looked after them a bit better.' He did it again. 'Ach! It's bloody hopeless.' He tipped the bottle between her lips and let slide a sluice of water. 'Won't need this if we are both fucking dead. I'm serious, God.' Suddenly, a great choking sound from Betty's chair. 'You trying to drown me, Albert?' He stared down at the crumpled, bubbling mess that was his late wife's friend. Truly, he stared through her to the chair that once was the repository of his wife. It was always 'her' chair. The weight of her body had been fashioned into the upholstery. The thought further unsettled him.

Doreen had slid down, her legs stretched out, heels as breaks so she did not finish up on the floor. Her bottom on the chair's edge, head and shoulders wedged against the chair's back, her hands on straightened arms tucked between her thighs. Her hair, though unkempt, had about it an air of

4

being coiffed, like a feature able to harbour a strong attraction. Dead, dying, seductive. Whatever, considered Albert, no fit state for any befitting female to find herself. She was covered in dust. Her cotton frock was patched with sweat. Its hem above her knees. 'Dear God, just look at the state of you … and that chain around your neck!' No wedding ring—that he could see. No stockings. Sanded sandals. Filthy feet. 'Are you wrecked or dead? Whichever, what do I do with you, you occupying Betty's chair?' Dribbles of water, wasted, dripped from her chin. 'I should save that!' He smiled. The dribbles had collected dust in their path to nowhere leaving routes streaked of chin-clean skin. War or plague. The downfall of the innocent. He stood back and observed Doreen from a little distance. 'Now that is a vulnerable person,' he said aloud. Then he looked at himself in the mirror. 'And this is another vulnerable person.'

*

Doreen is now sitting comfortably in Betty's chair. The hem of her cotton frock respectfully below her knees. Face wiped free from dust. A hunk of bread and cheese in her hand. A bottle of water within reach. Albert observing her. Thoughtful.

'Where's your old man, Doreen?'

'Dead. Didn't Betty tell you?'

'Betty didn't tell me anything about you. Just you lived by the railway station.'

'We met regular.'

'Regular. How regular?'

'Every week, Albert. Didn't Betty tell you?'

'Every week, you say, Doreen?'

'Yes, Albert. Always met by the thirty-nine bus stop before we went shopping.'

'You went by bus?'

'No, no, Albert. We just met there, and then walked. Didn't Betty tell you?'

'For God's sake don't keep asking if Betty told me. She told me nothing … except you lived by the bloody railway station!' Pause for thought. 'Where do you walk to, Doreen … when you went shopping?'

'To the Co-op.'

'Ah! The Co-op.' That sounded safe. He remembers seeing some of their labels on Betty's shopping.

'All day, was that, Doreen?'

'Lots of questions, Albert.'

'Betty never told me, Doreen.' Albert, though down, his brain was beginning to readjust, changing a gear and running more smoothly. He took a smidgen of delight to see that Doreen was uncertain how to answer, then felt guilty the whiff of suspicion should cross his mind when Betty had passed on—and Betty's friend occupied her chair.

'She came back to my place sometimes to have a rest and a cup of tea,' said Doreen. All matter-of-fact and quite calm, was Doreen.

'I always worked Wednesdays when Betty did her shopping. That's why she shopped on a Wednesday. Seemed to be a nice arrangement. Betty often said doing it like that I wouldn't get bored being left alone when she was out. But all day … Betty never told me that. Had tea with you, and a rest! And me with the forklift in the warehouse thinking she was at home nicely safe and sound.'

'Oh, Albert, she was nice and safe and sound when she came to tea. She would say: Albert will be pleased I'm here all safe and sound. He does worry for me ... when he can't see me.'

'She said that?'

'Yes, Albert, she said that.'

*

Albert was mindful. Was Doreen a poseur or a woman perhaps fearful of the onset of middle age and wrinkles, or simply an unloved woman in search of a last chance? He noticed she took pride in her hair: her crown, he thought. Spends money on its upkeep. Her unlined face suggested a maturity with experience, a confidence, but able to garner pity when necessary. Breasts that flourished without the sag of childbirth, a trim figure, tidy ankles—and only a little extra attention needed to attract. What made him think of street corners? But he did.

'How old are you, Doreen?'

'Now that's a funny question, Albert.'

'You just seem younger than my Betty, a good deal younger.'

'Well, I am younger. Nothing wrong with that, is there?'

'No, no. Just not quite right somewhere. That I never knew. Every week you say, and I never knew.' Albert began to hum the words of Love Me Tender. He stared at the recumbent figure in his late wife's chair. He should not have invited her to sit there. He considered asking her to move

7

into his, not feeling comfortable with such an immediate occupation of the chair that was only ever used by his late wife.

'I do like that song. I expect Betty played that to you. Made you feel all lovey-dovey and cuddly, wouldn't doubt.' Doreen gave Albert the first glimpse of a seductive, pasted-on theatrical smile that held no sincerity, was wafer-thin and soon vanished. He did not respond. She was possessed of the instinct gifted to attractive ladies to know when they are being appraised. When she was satisfied she stood up and announced she should be off home.

'See you tomorrow, if you like, Albert.'

*

Odd really, he thought. When I was married I think I would have liked that … a little bit of flirting coming my way to know I could rouse curiosity. Now I am single, and would be free from any impropriety, I'm not so sure.

He sensed the smell of the predator … if not predator then a sense of womankind exacting ascendency being temporarily down, or boredom wanting something different. To come in this heat, this dust, this bloody plague to his front door, something definitely not right. Betty's friend? Maybe. Apart from being a bag of bones she perked up no end once she had my sympathy. Not dead at all. Not even nearly dead at all. Skirt above her knees, coital position suggesting possibilities. Likely I'm imaging, just vulnerable and short on comfort. See you tomorrow, if you like, Albert. I should not have said that would be nice, Doreen. It just came out, unstoppable like. You should not have left me,

8

Betty. I should have gone first. Best I go out early tomorrow before the sun gets right up and scavenge for something to give her. Go down Fred's, if he's still there, and pay over the top for a couple of sausages, and find a few spuds. Bottled water at a premium. Might ask him if he knows Doreen. Butchers next to hairdressers to know people, or who know people who know people. More gossip, better the cut! He liked that. Butcher or hairdresser. Street corners and hairdressers, and now butchers! His thoughts should be on Betty not on the dwindling of small town incidentals.

The night after this different day he slept finding no guilt in his mind to keep him awake. As he dozed off he was aware that beside him Betty's place lay empty, as he had been aware every night since she died. He was aware of that, too, when he awoke the next morning—before thoughts of Doreen broke into his mind and took charge.

*

'Have you a couple of pork sausages, Fred, for a hungry man?' he said cheerfully.

'Losing weight like the rest of us, is it Albert?'

'Having to put extra holes in my belt to take up the slack,'

'Betty would not have liked that, would she? Put it down to her fault. Not feeding her man properly. Of course you miss her, Albert. Such a lovely lady. You were lucky. Mind you, she would not have wanted to see the town today. You would have not starved though: she would have seen to that!'

'Very practical, was my Betty. You're right there. I bet she could beat you down on the price of a couple of sausages,' he said with a touch of humour that made Fred smile.

'Didn't have to, mate. Too lovelier a person to give anything but the best deal. She knew that.'

Albert paid over the odds for his sausages. Fred knew he knew he had paid in excess, but friends can still become friends when times are hard. Fred could have said he was out of sausages. Albert, his mind now on finding potatoes, moved towards the butcher's door.

'I miss Betty on the piano, always was a crowd puller, wasn't she? You were a lucky man, Albert. So be thankful as well as sad,' Fred called out.

Crowd puller! His Betty? And he had forgotten to ask Fred about Doreen.

Albert popped his head back around the door.

'Forgot to ask you, Fred. Do you know a Doreen who lives by the railway station?'

'I'm probably not the only one, Albert.'

What did he mean by that? No, it can't be what it might mean, surely.

*

So we lose Albert for a while. The sun rises higher. The heat is beginning to readjust its temperature as it stretches out towards the uncomfortable. The dust stirs again after a night's rest. Potatoes are in short supply. Albert does not lose himself: his mind has lost cohesion. He is putting common parlance onto the bones of gossip, or is trying to, by running together the bits that unsettled him. Like …

… didn't Betty tell you? Oh, Albert, she was nice and

safe and sound when she came to tea. Always a crowd puller, wasn't she? Do you know a Doreen who lives by the railway station? I'm probably not the only one, Albert.

He searched potatoes for Doreen, and doubts about Betty. He wanted to find the first, but not the second.

*

See you tomorrow, if you like, Albert.

That would be nice, Doreen.

About lunchtime, Albert.

Okay, Doreen.

*

Albert mumbled, mumbled, mumbled away to himself. 'Only one way to clear my head is to ask Doreen. Not bloody possible my Betty played the piano in front of strangers on a Wednesday? Our house, or the pub on the corner by the railway station? I wouldn't have minded if she had told me. We told each other everything. That was the beauty of our marriage. No secrets, or that is what I thought. I'll know tomorrow. I'll ask that Doreen, straight. Not even a potato! Some back-handers shifting spuds to pigs. More profit in sausages. Well, the way Fred prices them there must be. I'm meant to be fucking bereaved and not out in the dust searching for spuds to feed some woman who lives by the railway station, and worrying what my Betty got up to when my back was turned. Betty, of all people! Thought I knew her inside out, back of my bloody hand. She never would. Love me tender? Always thought she did. Yet sometimes cool. Woman's prerogative. Tea always on the table when I came home from work. Even Wednesdays. Must have got it wrong. I'll give Doreen swedes instead.'

He is pleased when he reached home. Sanctuary. His world. Once it was his and Betty's. Now, just his—and dead. Gone with Betty. He looked at the piano. Imagined her there, her back ramrod straight, and the tilt of her head as she followed the notes. Christ, Betty dearest, I can still hear the music. 'I loved you,' he said aloud above its notes.

He spruced himself up. Prepared the swede. Placed the bottle of water, which he had kept in reserve, in the fridge. Sat in his chair. Could feel a tear rise. Got up when he noticed the dust on the table, became irresolute about removing it because by removing it the heart with its initials would have to go. But there was no way around that. He couldn't serve up sausages and swede on a dusty table. Plenty more dust where that came from. And in any case, Betty, forever my dear loved one, I shall draw a bigger and better heart next time. With a few quick swipes with a yellow duster he removed the dust and the heart from the table and sat back again in his chair satisfied he was prepared. He expelled half-a-dozen heavy breathes before setting his mind on the problems, which confronted him. He just needed time to think. Get them in order. He had questions to ask Doreen about Betty. He had questions to ask himself about Doreen. Wouldn't be able to ask them properly if Doreen has dressed herself in provocative clothing, like the stuff she was wearing yesterday. Didn't appear to him she was the sort of person who would arrive in a dowdy dress out of consideration for public decency, or his vulnerability. Mind you, could do with some genuine comfort, just holding a hand would be lovely.

The tap on the window was delivered assuredly. It echoed.

'God, you're keen,' he said, and went to let her in.

She was wearing a lightweight anorak with its hood over her head to keep out the dust, and carrying a shopping bag. The sun was at the midday. The impression was green. She looked neither hot nor flustered. She stood expectantly at the door before entering. Smiled. Stretched her neck, raised her lips for a kiss, and got one.

'Why, Albert, this is nice.'

'Yes, Doreen. Do come in.'

'I've brought you something … when I've taken off my anorak.'

'You shouldn't have, Doreen.'

'And why shouldn't I, Albert? You don't know what it is yet.' First out of the bag was a rather smart pair of comfy-looking green suede shoes. 'Much too nice to wear outdoors,' she said taking off her dusty sandals and brushing off the dust from her bare legs and ankles with slow, deliberate strokes. She straightened up and stretched herself to her full height, which must have been a good few inches less than five feet, in Albert's estimation. Her small feet. He noticed. Her frock was cotton, pale tangerine in colour and dropped loosely to fall short of her knees. Her hair—washed, rinsed and groomed by herself was untidily the fashion of the day. Her face a picture of sobriety, her whole person alert to whatever was available. She waited for Albert to register her attraction, which he did. She smiled. 'And this is what I have brought for you, Albert. I can tell you need feeding up. Some flapjack. Last of the oats. Betty told me it's one of your favourites.'

Albert puts on the chopped-up swedes to boil, and the sausages in the frying pan, slow. Doreen stands in the kitchen, nothing for her to do.

'Have a drink of water, Doreen, there's cold in the fridge.'

'Let me pour you one as well, Albert.'

'Thanks. Couldn't find any potatoes so I hope you like swedes, Doreen.'

'One of my favourites! So we both have our favourites then, Albert … my flapjack and your swede.' They laugh. She comes up close to him in front of the oven. They stare into the bubbling vegetable water and turn the sausages, are quiet, thoughtful. 'I expect you often helped Betty with the cooking. My man didn't get that side of marriage. Only was one side of marriage he could get, till he passed away. You and Betty cosy I expect, not like me and mine. Beer and you know what was all that interested him. Didn't do cosy and fireside chats. Didn't do children. He saw to that. Did the horses, mind you, if I gave him the cash. They were always dead-certs at the start and the never-winners at the end. He popped-it in bed with me … you know what I mean. Saved me on the funeral, Albert, because I reckon I'd already given him a good send off.' She smiled, and brushed her bare arm against his. 'He was a good man once, when I married him. My knight in shining armour. Kept the riff-raff away from me. I expect you got lots of sympathy when Betty passed away, but when my fella went people who knew us thought I had had a lucky escape.'

'Yes, Doreen, lots of sympathy when Betty went, but in time it's comfort one needs. Sympathy dilutes with time. All those sort of words spoken for, done ... done, and then comes the advice. And after that fucking nothing. Sympathy, advice and then the fucking nothing.' Albert stirs the swede. Doreen rolls the sausages gently ensuring the blacker ones are facing upwards. 'Apologies for my language, I do feel cross sometimes.'

'No, Albert, they call it bereavement.'

He feels a rising tear.

Doreen puts a hand on his shoulder.

It feels cool in the heat.

'Sad you didn't have any kids, Albert. Betty said you would have made a lovely Dad.'

*

Plates wiped clean. Two empty glasses that once held water. A moment when time pauses to give opportunity for humans to speak, to release what is on their minds, awaiting a favourable opportunity. This was Albert's. He grabbed the empty time.

'Doreen, did Betty often go back to your place for a cup of tea after shopping on a Wednesday?'

'Most times, Albert. Then not so often when you stopped work. Why do you ask?'

'Because she never told me.' Pause. 'Did she ever play the piano ... to other people?'

'That's a funny question, Albert. How would I know that?'

'Just that Fred said he missed Betty playing the piano.'

15

'Did Fred say that? Well, I really can't say.'

A touch of discomfort. Albert noticed. Doreen's eyes looked away, down.

'Do you have a piano?'

'Goodness me, no! With my fella you just had beer and the horses. Money for a piano! Never. Anyway, who would have played it?'

'Betty.'

'Betty didn't have to. She had one of her own.' She pointed a finger over her shoulder at the upright. 'Over there.' Tetchy. Too many questions. Albert switched.

'Let's sit on the comfy chairs. I'll clear the table. Not much to clear. Sign of the times, and our little world being turned upside down. Money making more money. Of those without being more without. If we had had kids they would have been able to help us, wouldn't they Doreen?'

'We can help ourselves, Albert.'

'How do you mean, Doreen?'

Doreen was now sitting back in Betty's chair. Albert was in the kitchen putting away the few things. He boiled a kettle.

'Cup of tea, Doreen?' he called out.

'That would be nice, Albert. I'll share a lump of sugar with you. Tie a bit of cotton around it so we can dangle it in our cups.'

'How long you been on your own, Doreen?'

'Not long enough.'

'That's a bit harsh.'

'You didn't have to live with him! Mind you, Albert, I didn't for a few years. But I had to agree he could have what

he reckoned was his matrimonial right ... if he was that desperate, and he left me in peace to live my own life. Always
gave him money. I paid his debts ... right to the end.'

'When was his end, Doreen?'

'Must be two years now.'

'Betty never told me.'

'She never liked him. Said I should have divorced him
rather than give way to his demands. Didn't really know
him. Just a brute, Albert, just a brute.' She fell silent,
thoughtful. 'Not like you, Albert, I can tell.'

*

So reader, we are in Number Seven, in a downstairs room
in a town struggling to survive because no rain has fallen
for as long as most can remember. Dust is choking life and
business. The sun burns. The black market has been rife.
Survival is the prerogative of the fittest. Without the occasional charitable-bottled-water all life would have gone. Yet
there is hope. A distant generator continued to pump power
down its cables. Someone far adrift either did not know—
or did care. For sure the dead would not be able to pay
their bills. Power was not expected to be sustained, and it
seemed a miracle no distant finger had already flicked the
switch. Time passes. It is approaching teatime. Albert and
Doreen sit opposite each other. Albert in his chair: Doreen
in Betty's. There is a sense neither wish to close down their
solitude. If Albert is honest he does not want Doreen to
go. She takes his mind away from loss and loneliness. He
is cocooned, held in place by a powerful magnet that both
attracts and repels, persistently. He sees Doreen, woman-

kind with instincts suggestive of a calculated involvement, an emotional algorithm capable of enticement, of fascination, of being able to provide a need—on her terms. Yet, there is an air of contentment afloat in periods of weighty silence when to break it would be presumptuous. The ticking of a clock would be music, the steadiness of it reflecting the mood. It would be wrong to assume that predator and prey faced each other, waiting their next moves. Both were predators and both were prey. It was the silence. It was the nothingness that heralded a tomorrow. The dust. The heat. The silence. It was not the end of the big, wide world, only did each harbour the impression it was the end of theirs. Their town was doomed. Folk were being left to die. The rich were scooping up what was left and were off, through the rising dust—gone. Albert and Doreen could get off at separate stops, or hold on to what was left of the ride together. Albert with his sleeves rolled, examining his hands as if the answer lay in the dust beneath his fingernails. And Doreen, while eyeing him, runs a finger slowly along the hem of her dress.

'How did you make the money, Doreen, to keep your man in beer and horses?'

The bolt. The silence broken.

'Serving in the pub, mostly.'

'Serving? You mean pulling pints?'

'Yes, Albert, something like that.' Albert went back to examining his hands.

'Betty with you sometimes, when you were pulling pints, was she?'

'Yes, Albert.'

'On a Wednesday, Doreen?'

'Yes, Albert, on a Wednesday.'

'Just the Wednesdays, Doreen?'

'Yes, Albert.'

'In the pub?'

'Yes, Albert.'

'Not at your place?'

'No, Albert.'

'All nice and safe and sound then, on a Wednesday, as you said.' Doreen not slow to pick up on the drift. Tightened up, in defensive mode now. Her finger ceased to caress the hem of her dress.

'Now don't spoil it, Albert, we're having such a nice time.'

'Just want to know, Doreen, that's all.'

'Not much to know. Betty helped me ... that's all. I needed help. I needed money to get my man off my back.'

'How did she help you, Doreen?'

'She played the piano while I served the punters.'

'Served?' Albert raised his eyebrows.

'You know what I mean, Albert.'

'I'm not sure I do, Doreen.'

'Well, Albert, there is more than one way to skin a cat, and more than one way to pull a beer, or a punter.' Doreen inflected a lighter tone beneath a shadowy smile.

'Pulling, Doreen, was that it?' said Albert sharply. 'And now the punters are all gone here you are. And my Betty gone too. I just need to know.'

'She would have told you if there was anything to tell.'

'I don't think so, Doreen. Not if she was ashamed, or

something.'

'So on a Wednesday afternoon she played the piano while I pulled in the punters. Goodness me, Albert, we were in the pub. She never left the piano, that's all there was to it.'

'You worked as a team?'

'Yes, Albert we worked as a team.'

'What sort of music did she play?'

'Oh, just the smoochy sort. Some folk liked to dance.'

'The kiss and cuddly sort of music, Doreen?'

'Yes, that was the idea. It turned them on, relaxed them. They looked forward to Wednesdays.'

'Like ... Love Me Tender ...?'

'Yes, Albert. That was one of the favourites.'

'It was our song.'

'Yes, Albert. Betty told me.'

'She did?'

'Yes, Albert. When she played it her face lit-up like. All the wrinkles gone. Beautiful eyes, seeing. Miles away she would be. I thought, how lovely it must be to love a man like that ... for it to be so real that it shone.'

'You thought that, Doreen?'

'Yes, Albert, I did.' Albert continued to study his hands, for a while. There was a tear waiting somewhere in the back of his left eye. He looked across at Doreen, motionless, save her finger was running slowly again along the hem of her dress.

'It's all gone now, Albert. The pubs closed, punters gone, Betty gone, our town has damn near gone ... and tomorrow you and I may be gone. Right now we could be the only ones alive in this street. When did you last see anyone around here? Albert, you just tell me that. When did you?'

'What you mean, we could be gone tomorrow?'

'For Christ's sake Albert, we'll either be dead, or we'll be dragging ourselves along the dust-filled ruts made by the cars of the rich as they haul away what is probably not theirs. I got to know some of the men on a Wednesday when their wives were elsewhere, out drinking tea from cups and saucers, or whatever the posh do to amuse themselves. I can tell you Albert, the men aren't nice, aren't nice at all, but they had the money, cash up front.'

'I don't know what to say.'

'Don't say anything, Albert. Have you got anything to drink? Save the water, alcohol will do?' Doreen flashed a smile. 'Never thought I'd hear myself say that!'

'Got some cherry brandy left over from last Christmas, Doreen.'

'Wow! That's a drink I love.'

They stand up. Doreen straightens her frock, pulls it down. It doesn't reach her knees, though she seemed surprised it did not. They go into the kitchen and Albert shoves his arm into the deep recess of an empty cupboard and produces, like a magician, a bottle part-filled with cherry brandy.

'There! We must have been keeping this bit for something.'

'Let's share a glass then, Albert.' Albert looks doubtful. 'We can just sip, sip, sip. See the old world out together.'

Albert carries the bottle and the one glass. Doreen draws the curtains, switches on the standard lamp that stands by the piano and moves the two chairs side-by-side. Close to touching. They sit gazing into the empty grate. Albert pours. They each take a sip. The sun has had its day. The heat is cooling. There is the sense that no life exists outside. Just the two of them sitting in the quiet, thinking. Doreen stretches out a hand for Albert to take. He looks at it. It has come from Betty's chair. It is a small, comforting hand, well-meaning. Would Betty mind, if he held it—just for a while? All this may be gone tomorrow. He takes hold of it. It's cool, gives, tucks into his. There is an emotion. He feels the vibes, a tremor of something. He gently squeezes. There is a response. Comfort. They sip.

'Betty never did what I had to do. She never had to. You know why, Albert? I'll tell you. Because you're a good man, a loving husband.'

Silence.

The light flickers.

'You're right, Doreen, the lights are going out. Some bugger has found the switch. I have a candle.'

'I don't think we'll need a candle.'

'Why not?'

'We can feel the bottle and glass.'

*

The lights go out. The glass put aside. And the bottle empty. It could be midnight. Albert has lit the candle. Doreen is leading the way up the stairs. There was more cherry brandy in the bottle than Albert realised. No matter. It was all gone. No words. An understanding? Hard to tell. A predator and its prey—or two predators? The candle is placed on Betty's

22

dressing table. Albert has poured wax onto the wood surface and fixed the candle upright into the wax. The dressing table mirror reflects the light across the room. Albert watches as Doreen undresses. The kicking off of the shoes, deliberate. The first move. The stepping out of the pale tangerine frock. A pile on the floor. The bra. The pants. That order. Albert noticed. Women all the same, he imagined. Doreen lies back on the bed. Albert has not moved, one hand is steadying him on the edge of the dressing table.

'Come on then, Albert. What are you waiting for?'

Albert moves closer.

He is looking down at the naked woman where once his Betty lay. In the flickering light of the candle Doreen's attractiveness made her appear to him a thing of beauty. Although the Betty with whom he had lived for so many years was perhaps not as beautiful—for sure she was good-looking and had an attraction that ridiculed this woman whose nakedness lay staring up at him. Such ridicule negated the comfort for which he desperately wished. He threw over the duvet to cover it up.

'Just going downstairs for a moment, Doreen.'

He eased the candle from the wax, lit his way back down the stairs.

He collected from the piano the music for Love Me Tender, extinguished the candle, slipped quietly out of the front door of Number Seven and set off westwards in the direction of the cemetery, humming.

The Photograph

In the boardroom of an international fashion house Guy Svelte, its Chairman, stood up and cleared his throat. The members of the Board noted these gestures, adjusted their ears to pay extra attention, and alerted their bodies into mindful mode because their future may depend on it. For years Guy Svelte had inflicted upon his stomach quantities of the best food money could buy. His name had now ceased to be analogous to his physique. When he had first come to work at the fashion house he may well have been willowy and attractive to an osier, but with success and power came the rigours of obesity. Across the globe he was fondly referred to as the Dumpling. What was strange he cited his obese opulence, but not in so many ways, as an example of what any employee of his company can become by dedication and loyalty even if they start at the very bottom—as he had. He was very interested in the young. And he understood the importance of the base of a pyramid. He had the longest way to fall if it crumbled.

Guy Svelte looked at the members of his Board. Male and female members sat in equal numbers, which was one of his early aspirations on gaining the chairmanship. He had a fondness for all of them. Many had reached maturity under his guidance and he had a patriarchal feeling about their well-being. He had kept them neither sufficiently affluent so not to seek employment elsewhere, nor sufficiently rich to feel overconfident and irreplaceable. They were his children. His wife had failed to give him any. If any of the them had criticism of their father-figure it was he was just too nice in a business world corrupted by power, deceit and commercial theft. But he had survived, and his fashion house flourished.

They listened, and their Chairman began:

'Every year we take on employees to replace natural wastage. Here in our European offices, for example, we take on twenty or so. Each has been skimmed from the top of the very best by selection, but I wonder what their minds absorb when not enjoying the limelight of their own brilliant and versatile moments, and whether this absorption is dependent on the spongy comfort zones where they were weaned. Somewhere between their brilliance and versatility there may lie innovations that a nudge might expand into fresh ideas and exotic designs. I want to open up these ideas before they become distorted by commercial considerations. Viewing what is new through tinted spectacles is what our new arrivals need to avoid, and they should not be dazzled by fashion's lassitude and complacency. I am minded to ask each to suggest a way of holding people's attention so they take more than a single glance at us, and having glanced are prepared to keep open their eyes on our products in the future. I want people's minds to empty, then reflect and remember us. I want their attention held while their brains stow generous thoughts. I want to hold their attention. How do you hold someone's attention in a world that is a busy place? Capturing minds must surely have a degree of finesse, some subtlety and an insight into the psyche of human rationale. Blatancy can sometimes appear ugly and crude in our profession. I would like to ask each recent arrival to produce, say within one month, a short appraisal outlining their ideas to persuade people to think of us whenever they think of fashion. Simply, I want the world to love us, to love *Hofus* ... the House of Us.'

And the Board nodded, and agreed to give European prominence to the best idea.

*

Fredric Jeremiah Jokes lived with his mother in Surbiton. He had no brothers or sisters. His mind was acute, fuelled by an instinct that observed the happenings in accordance with the ordinary course of nature and their relationship to street life, survival and emotional ambiguities. He absorbed facts like a sponge. He understood and drew out from the success of others undoubted pleasure. He had an intellectual view of beauty and design, and the rounded knowledge of worldly art and its derivations. He had a discreet eye for the unobscured. And yes, he had the letter from Europe for which he had waited some days, but had concealed from his mother for fear she would either cry or become excessively jubilant. He found a day when the matter would be the least demanding on his unassuming nature.

'Have you told your father yet?'

'No.'

'It's lovely news. He will be proud of you.'

'It is you he should be proud of, Mum. You have fed and clothed me, and allowed me freedom.' His mother spread wide her arms and took unto herself the son she cherished, and who was all she had. Her eyes glistened with tears.

'A job in *Hofus* ... for my Fredric! Oh, I'm going to walk so tall today, and every day from now on. You know, darling, you have the eyes for beauty just like your grandmother. And you have her vision of what is best and what is kindest for everyone. Oh, how I wish she were here to see you now! You are going to dress the world! And from *Hofus*.' She continued to hug him.

'It is a foot on the bottom rung, that is all, Mum. The office tea boy.'

'You will rise, darling. You'll make the very best tea. You're sensitive ... and that's what they need in the rag trade. And what was that quote by Coco Chanel? The best things in life are free. The second best are very expensive. You told me that. Do you believe that, now you are going where things are likely to be very expensive?' Fredric rubbed gently his mother's shoulder, and took pleasure from her delight at his success. He broke free from her embrace, and stood back.

'Of course, yes. I should love to design and make the primitive instinctive forces in a person feel free ... that are not constrained by pattern or thought.'

'Like the little black dress?'

'Yes, Mum.'

'Go phone your Dad ... just for me.'

'Yes, Mum.'

*

27

Well, of course, that afternoon out came the family photographs. His mother spread them on the table, faces from history stared up. She made a point of selecting the photographs of her mother and herself wearing outfits his grandmother had designed and made. Some of the outfits were age-proof and appropriate, and looked good. His mother always loved to show him the collection of the family photographs, and to elaborate the lives of those who had gone before, or who were still alive, but had become invisible. Fredric gazed earnestly at the photographs (he had seen them quite a few times) knowing how much his mother wanted him take an interest. He refreshed his memories of many.

*

Fredric arrived at the head office of the European arm of *Hofus* at Rüdesheim on the Rhine at the appointed time. He was lightly dressed as the day was hot. Whether or not it was so, he sensed the aroma of wine in the pretty town as a traveller to Gouda might sense the aroma of cheese. Off the streets and into the *Hofus* modern offices there was a different atmosphere—it was crisp, cool, marbled clean and quietly expeditious. Views across the Rhine with its steady barges moving effortlessly gave Fredric an impression of national functionality. He was expected. A Fräulein with assured composure and the looks of a Nordic goddess greeted him, confirmed he was expected: further she would escort him, when he was refreshed if he so needed to be, to the office of the Chairman who would personally welcome him.

So, Reader, we have a young and uninitiated man intro-
duced into the office of a man who had his finger on the
pulse of a beating fashion empire. This man had a rotund
figure topped by a genial face. Whereas Fredric was yet too
unworldly to perceive behind this relaxed, welcoming and
open façade a man with a camouflaged astuteness that the
arrogant failed to appreciate at their peril. Guy Svelte stood
up from behind his desk and then there occurred one of
those intangible actions that bedevil human rationale, he
opened wide his arms to Fredric Jeremiah Jokes and hugged
him.

'I welcome you to the House of Us, to become one of us.'
Then he sat down. 'Please sit. I have your file here. I have
read it. I thank you for placing your trust in us by wishing
to come here … and for accepting gracefully our methods,
which can be considered draconian by those lacking resolve,
in our selection procedure. So I say 'welcome' Fredric.

'You will be allocated a position within the company
after a month or so when you will have seen what we do,
both men's and ladies' fashions, and we can evaluate how
best you can serve us. But first I should like you to take a
look at this office and describe to me what you see. This
is not some kind of initiation, I can assure you. It is just I
like to take in how quickly you can assemble in your mind,
without warning, what you see before you. Descriptive
analysis, if you like.'

Fredric collected his thoughts. He was never one to be
hurried. If it was a virtue it was a virtue that often irri-
tated his mother. Time for her was seldom spacious. He did
not survey the office, but gazed with a contemplative mind

upon the Chairman.

'My first impression as I entered your office, Sir, was how light and airy it was, and how the blinds controlled the light. Then before you I noticed the large desk that was clear of all but an intercommunication system, a photograph frame, my file and a pencil probably made from incense cedar. The office is uncluttered. There are no pictures on the walls, there is a small area set aside with comfy seats and a coffee table with a marble top that is probably Italian where associates may relax. The wall colour is a dusty pastel green. The flooring is laid with oak that has been brushed and oiled. The whole arguably fashionless, which is strange. There is no waste paper basket.'

'Thank you Fredric. Yes, it is uncluttered. Here I give myself space to reflect. In this office, which is empty of distraction, I find space for ideas to germinate. There is a matter I have to put before you. The Board has agreed to ask each new arrival to produce a short appraisal outlining an idea that could persuade people to think of *Hofus* whenever they think of fashion. Simply, it wants the world to love us. Could you put together something for me to see that I can ask the Board for comments? Would one month be sufficient time?'

Guy Svelte stood up, held out his hand to be shaken, and opening the door led out Fredric Jokes for departure.

*

Fredric Jokes returned to Surbiton and surprised his mother. He explained to her that he was on a personal project required by Mr Svelte himself. He remembers seeing a photograph of her, which he would like borrow. She was delighted that one of her may be going to *Hofus*! She spread the photographs across the table and watched her son through eyes registering love and pride—more, the desire to hold tight her son. Fredric rummaged. She gazed in wonder. Both were intense about their thoughts that came from distinct and differing pools. Fredric raised his hand, pointed a hovering finger at one of the photographs and declared:

'This one!' His finger descended slowly onto one depicting a lady in front of some steps.

'That's me, darling!' she explained.

'I know, Mum, and it is the one I would like to borrow.'

*

The photograph had been taken twenty-five years before with a camera, which possessed no great distinction or sense of practical aspiration. It was a photograph snapped on the spur of the moment and taken to express a fleeting passage of time—and destined for the family album whose need lay in viewings during the years to come.

*

The photograph: *A young lady in her prime is stepping forward, and is thoughtful. She is about to take the first step of a semi-circular flight made from pale, marbled pink stone leading upwards to an open arena nearing completion. The ascent is suggestive of fresh, unclimbed stone, and thus undiscovered. There is colour in the picture: it is subtle and not dominant. The reddish-brown hair of the lady silhouetted in front of the pale, marbled pink sweep of the steps catches the eye. There is a green* *fusion of foliage integrated by the builders on the perimeter of the site to reflect not-forgotten Nature, which mitigates any harshness of the practical slabs that may be used above the steps. The earring of gold suspended beside the auburn hair sparkles, but does not distract from the un-orchestrated photograph.*

An enlargement is the basis for the poster through which Fredric Jeremiah Jokes will illuminate his idea to make the world love *Hofus*. He will need to tweak the photograph to erase any paper-copy imperfections, and to exactly place the *Hofus* logo where it will be most effective.

He has an expansive and pathless notion to see his poster hung in Milano Centrale railway station. When asked why—he considered men of Italian blood would best detect its hidden beauty.

*

Chairman Svelte has returned from China where his trip has confirmed the strong position in which his company finds itself. He is in a tranquil frame of mind. In his uncluttered office, and free from distraction, he awaits with a benign interest for Fredric Jokes to enter. He has settled down to listen, learn and measure in his mind the calibre of this recent employee, and is hoping for something innovative and creative—and articulated in an easy flow.

A screen has been prepared onto which his poster can be attached.

With it rolled beneath his arm, he enters.

'Good morning, Sir.'

'Good morning, Fredric. I hope you have something congenial for me.'

'I should like to think so, Sir. If something is simple it compliments congeniality. And if simplicity is the ultimate sophistication, in words by Leonardo da Vinci, then I would wish my idea to be satisfyingly simple ... and congenial.' Chairman Svelte nodded, accepting the quote as a preludial mechanism. 'If I may put up my realistic yet analogical poster, I hope to show you my thoughts on the task the Board has set me.' Chairman Svelte readjusted his frame a little, settled back. He liked this young man. He was uncertain exactly why. It is the prerogative of the up and coming to be in some manner pleased with themselves, and Fredric Jeremiah Jokes was modestly pleased with himself. He was able to arrange answers that would appear to exceed the capabilities of many of similar age. But he was still a young man limited by experience. Chairman Svelte understood this and did not feel an aversion for it.

'I am keen to hear what you have come up with so it might be placed for consideration before the Board,' he said benignly.

'Let us imagine two people gazing at my poster,' began Fredric. 'Both of their attentions have been held. Each is the proverbial man-in-the-street ... one hovers on the perimeter of fashion and is aware of its benefits, and is not controlled by it, and the other is also aware of the benefits, but is controlled by it. We need to encourage the first, and hold on to the second. We need to take them off the street, metaphorically, and to love us. The poster aims to capture their cognitive thoughts, and to place in their receptive memories the word *Hofus*.' Fredric fixes his poster to the top of the screen and gently allows it to roll open. He follows the chairman's eyes as they range across it.

'About twenty-five years ago they were building like that, I should guess. And what the young lady is wearing, and even her demeanour, would also suggest that,' offered Chairman Svelte leaning back in his chair.

'Quite so, Sir. But to me it is a timeless frame. As fresh today as it was a quarter of a century ago. There is balance and poise, and industry. It holds the attention of those who at first glance at it, then pause for a longer look. It is magnetic, for no instant reason. Yet further study of it drip feeds, as it were, tantalising snippets, which are absorbed.' He points to the poster while explaining each facet—the reddish-brown hair, the flight of virgin steps, the fusion of green foliage, the sparkling earring, the lady in her prime who is thoughtful and on the ascendency. Fredric continues. 'Sir, it is a poster inviting thought, and reflection … and the expectation of the good things to come. The lady is fashion-enlightened in a simple way. A lasting way. An affordable way. Could she become everyone's dream of a next door neighbour? Could such a poster become iconic without trying to be so? It is saying something. Different minds may translate a different message, but minds will remember. They will and hopefully come to the same conclusion … entrancing, and from there it is but a short step for our two proverbial men to wonder what this poster is all about. The logo, like the fashion house it represents, is not brazen. It has been placed delicately on the poster and gives them a sense of success to have located it in the bottom corner, behind the lady's tread. She has absorbed it and is carrying it forward. To the men-in-the-street I hope *Hofus* will always be synonymous with the lady with the auburn hair who they wish lived next door ... and who carries the distinct message from which they will always think *Hofus*, love *Hofus*, buy *Hofus*.'

*

Guy Svelte is silent. He is taking a very careful look at Fredric Jokes's poster. There is the perception of a smile, kindly. Also the perception of a businessman's approach to an idea that could deliver. Iconic—fleets across his mind— entrancing. Yes, that too! So up he stands, comes around his big desk and rests a fatherly hand on Fredric's shoulder.

'Where would you see this poster displayed?' he asks.

'On a wall of naked brick.'

'But where, Fredric, where? Which naked wall?'

'On a wall at Milano Centrale railway station.'

A pause.

'I am acquainted with the President of the Grandi Stazi- oni. It might be arranged,' responded Guy Svelte with a modest tap on Fredric's shoulder. 'Do you love this lady?'

'Yes, Sir.'

'Who is she?'

'My mother.'

'Then you are both exceedingly fortunate.'

The Promissory Note

The essential treasures gifted on this Earth are Mothers and Friends. It is not possible to be without the first, and without the second life cannot be enriched.

Prioritising other gifts bring home to roost the disagreeable consequences of disappointment.

A Mother is laden with nourishment and tenderness, and is a fortress against misfortune. Friends, of which there may be many and who may lodge in the shell-scrapes of humanity, can be transient by Nature and fickle without the ties of blood—yet, amongst the swamps of these often avaricious and self-concerned folk it is possible to stumble upon a treasure who can sit alongside a Mother in thought and deed, and become a lifelong blessing and steely prop.

It is about two such Friends that I am privileged to write.

*

Geronimo Giles is a young man of soft hued wit and bred into poverty

and

Savannah Abascal is a lady with business acumen and Iberian temperament.

*

As is the case of every chance meeting Geronimo and Savannah met not by premeditated hope, not by design, not by exploration, not for gain or self-enhancement, but by the drift of life—and an acknowledgement that in spite of political injustices the world was a beautiful place. The zephyr of bored optimism drifted over them. The rubble of war-torn Europe had been their birthright until a quiet peace arose amongst the dust and destruction—and Savannah followed the homing of a white dove.

Where to start? Probably best when Savannah said to her mother and father:

'*Que sera sera*,' and headed north. A blue sky beckoned beneath the olive groves. Cart tracks ground the centuries of soil. Scattered workers, dotted here and there in their white shirts, gave order to her first steps in search of personal space. 'One day at a time,' she said to herself, 'then I shall always arrive.' She walked, she worked—she took her time, opportunely a bus ride, but never a train or plane. A creature of Nature. She crossed the Pyrenees, placed one foot in France, kept one in Spain: paused. She had left her home: now she had to decide to leave her country. Less of a wrench, but both set stolid in spite of the vagaries of Man. She lay back, closed her eyes, letting the mountain breeze torment the sun that played on her face. And across this playground a shadow passed to and fro alerting her—to she knew not what. On a branch of a pine tree settled a pure white dove. Up there it looked tiny. It was tiny. It fluttered its wings.

'*Mi palomita blanca. Mi hermosa palomita blanca.*'

My beautiful little white dove. She called to it, held out her hand and it flew down and settled on her palm. She stroked it gently and said:

'You must be a messenger from God ... you decide which way.'

She continued to stroke it and to talk to it.

And the bird stretched out its wings.

'*De que manera, mi hermosa?*'

Which way, my beautiful?

And she followed it northwards into France.

It flew ahead. And when it did not fly ahead it would sit on her shoulder or she would place it in an outer pocket of her backpack so that its tiny head could peep out.

Northwards across the Massif Central they travelled. The months travelled with them. Where Savannah lingered, where she stayed awhile to work, she became known as *la dame à la colombe*.

They reached the Channel. The ferry, the gulls, the concentration of commerce.

She scattered sunflower seeds, and boarded the ferry alone. She watched the little bird peck and search for the seeds, she watched it as the ferry sailed, she watched until its whiteness became a distant speck on a foreign shore until it, too, vanished.

*

Geronimo had a compass. His intention was to travel westwards until he reached the sea. He had looked at the map in the public library gleaning from it the place where he would cross Offa's Dyke and stride with triumph into Wales. He, too, would walk and work, his time being ample and he without personal concern. His father had moved on, moved out within a week of his birth. When he became aware his name caused adult folk to raise their eyebrows and his peers to snigger he asked his mother why it was he was called a name not associated with the industrial town in which he had been bred—his mother had replied, bluntly:

'You was all red when you was born so your father called you Geronimo after some red Indian he'd heard of. Then he slammed the door and was gone.'

So Geronimo said farewell to his mother on the doorstep of the tenement that had been his only home (and temporary home for his other fathers) for all his years. His mother, though relieved to see the back of him because she would have more space to accommodate her acquaintances and less explaining to do, could not withhold a certain dampness about her eyes. He was a good-looking boy, and if she were honest with herself, would miss the compliments that came with him.

'Where you making for, Gero?' She would call him that in rare moments of closeness.

'Wales, Mam. Don't worry ... shan't send you any scalps, Welsh much too nice for that.'

Then Geronimo saw the tear. It trickled ever so slowly down her cheek, reluctantly as if she sought pity. It carried with it a spark of tenderness to be remembered, a gift to be borne. It went with him up and over Offa's Dyke, it rested where he rested, it worked where he worked in places with unpronounceable names, and then along the mountain road dotted white with flannel sheep. It would, in time, see the sea. But first Geronimo came to a place to pause, to an unexpected attraction tucked away where the mountain road began its steady decline amongst the lower foothills. A signpost gave hint of its existence. A disused lead mine where visitors could have an insight into a way of life long gone. A hot food trader sold fast food and drinks from a converted caravan. A few tables and chairs nestled nearby. Ramshackle, weather-beaten, an extraneous complex, a trekker's oasis from which odours from a frying breakfast (though it was midday) emitted. At first it appeared to Geronimo to be an adjunct of the mine—another source of income to take advantage of a market where any other competition would be out of sight beyond the next set of hills. But there it was, an inviting carbuncle close to the faded brick and slate, tired buildings of the old mine. Low cloud restricted the sun. The weather was mild, with a faint suggestion of dampness. As Geronimo made his way towards the caravan he was struck by the quietness, the lack of human activity, nothing much seemed to be going on, save the smell of frying there being a strange dreamlike quality about what he had stumbled upon.

Savannah, solitary, sat waiting for her breakfast.

*

No other being was visible to Geronimo, save the proprietor, the entrepreneur with his frying pan alive amongst the vacant Welsh foothills. Geronimo ordered sausages, bacon, eggs, beans and a cup of tea. While this was being cooked he looked around and the proprietor engaged him in polite conversation.

'Come far?'

'England.'

'First time here?'

'Yes.'

'Where you making for?'

'Just the sea.'

'Well, you've almost made it. Long way to come for a swim.' The proprietor smiled, prepared on a tray a plate with sausages and bacon and a slice of bread and butter. Placed beside it a bottle of juice and carried it out to the lone girl. Geronimo watched him. His sausages began to spit in the frying pan. The proprietor returned.

'Foreign,' he said nodding towards where the girl sat. 'Bit like you. Lots of you about these days. University students.' He rolled the sausages over. 'Landladies love them. Well, we all do I suppose. If they weren't here I'd have to tow my caravan to the M4 ... but then it would never get that far!' Another roll of the sausages. Bacon prepared. The smell of frying inviting.

'Where would you like to sit?'

Geronimo, although he had already decided, gave pretence that it was not a matter of great concern.

'The table next to the girl will do fine,' he said, pointing.

The proprietor opened the palms of his hands indicating: Well, who wouldn't. And with the oral tradition of a bard he said:

'In this land of *hiraeth* yearning is cradled.' And with that the proprietor carried Geronimo's tray and placed it on the table next to Savannah's.

*

It was inevitable. Strangers in a strange land. The proprietor eyed them with the keenness of a theatre buff at the rising of the curtain on a first night. Two figures on an empty stage. They smiled politely as folk do if they are sharing the same space. Looked down, ate, looked up, caught the other's eye, understood the setting was surreal because no conscious effort could have affected how they found themselves where they were—like being washed up on a desert island only to find to find a gentleman serving late breakfasts! Geronimo broke the ice.

'You come far?' he asked good-naturedly.

'Spain.'

'I'm from England.'

They looked down, continued with their breakfasts.

'My aim is to reach the sea,' said Geronimo cheerfully.

'I'm enjoying some personal space.' Savannah's English was good, pleasantly accented.

'No final destination?'

'No. That is the fun of it. Time no problem. Walk. Work and walk again … *asi*, so here I am.' Savannah continued to tuck into her breakfast.

An aura of respect established itself, hung over them, began to remove initial uncertainty from reticence.

'Which way are you going next?'

Savannah pointed vaguely towards where Geronimo understood the sea lay waiting.

'Maybe now I look for a piece of civilization. Just for a

time. Find a job and a comfy bed!'

'I'm just following my compass westwards. When I find the sea I stop … and send a postcard home to my Mam. Anyway, I am Geronimo from England, and like you searching for a bit of space.'

'I am Savannah. No shortage of space here!'

They smiled, licked their plates clean.

He had an edge on him, which she liked.

And they didn't come like her the other side of Offa's Dyke.

*

So it was in the most unlikely of places these two travellers met in a foreign land. They sat on the scorched landscape of culture and heritage, they devoured their breakfasts as they would over the years devour that moment, their moment amongst the sloping hills that stretched to the sea. Like the cast-on stitch of a knitted garment their lives would grow together stitch by stitch, row by row, making a garment for life, which would be effortlessly dedicated, patterned with integrity and unsung blessings—flannel against the wet and windy winters of life.

*

They pitched their tents side-by-side. Two days and two nights to reach the sea. No hurry. Friendship not attracted to pace: better the steady pulse of conversation slowly navigating a celestial route. Of the white shirts of the olive grove workers, the white dove with its sense of direction, the sheep white with their unsheared flannel, even the caterer's caravan once white now spattered with uncared for dirt—these 'whites' of time and distance now joined by the white crests of the waves that rolled in across Cardigan Bay to reach landfall at their very feet.

Boarding houses aplenty. Traditional in times of holiday resorts, but now bread and butter for the landladies serving needs of university students.

'Here, this looks good,' said Geronimo. Vacancies says the sign. A bay tree in a pot stood sentinel at a front door that looked polished clean with tidy bricks leading up to it. They knocked at number 55. A motherly figure sized them up.

'You not off the train, then?' she queried.

'No. We have walked,' said Savannah. 'We are looking for two single rooms.'

'For how long?'

'That depends … if we find jobs. If not for a couple of weeks,' put in Geronimo.

'Not students, then?'

'No. Travellers.'

Now Mrs G Morgan (widow) has her reputation to uphold. Taking in 'travellers' not like university students with education, student loans, and university powers-that-be if things go wrong. She looked them up and down again.

'Pets?' This gave her time to think.

'We have no pets. I had a dove from the Pyrenees that came with me across France, but I left it there when I boarded the ferry.' This went a wee bit over Mrs Morgan's head, but she got the drift. There was nothing 'put on' with these two, they were robust and handsome in their own

44

way. Honest-looking faces. She always prided herself she could tell by paying especial attention to callers' faces.

'Two single rooms,' you said. 'Would you like to see them before we discuss terms?' She opened the door wide enough for them to get their backpacks and slung tents passed the posts without touching the paintwork.

Nice rooms. Close. Terms agreed. They hugged (the first time) to celebrate a unified success.

'Fish and chips?'

'Why not!'

They found a bench on the sea front. Strollers passed both ways. The tidal shifts made music as the waves strummed the pebbles. The air was different. Salt-laden suggesting health-giving. As Geronimo and Savannah tucked into their fish and chips a feeling of well-being came over them as reality dawned they had made landfall. And the company each offered the other felt extraordinarily genial sensing their temperaments must have much in common to be at ease on the same bench so far from home. There were spells of enjoyed silence when they glanced at each other, devouring their meal with greasy fingers, almost guiltily, and smiled—being quite thoughtful of their circumstances.

*

They found work in the same hotel. Mrs Morgan called them single-sleepers. She liked them. They were not work-shy; clean they were with tidy frames of mind and above all seemingly (and she could tell!) wholesomely chaste. Interested in her, too, they were often offering to help, nothing too much trouble, a pleasure to have around. So she was crestfallen when Savannah said she was moving on, continuing northwards on her travels. But she would return, sometime. Geronimo would stay on. He had reached his destination, found the sea, indicated he would stay on for a while. He gave her his compass in case the clouds conceal the north star—excusing his generosity, but wanting her to carry a token of remembrance of the compassion they had discovered together.

'*Amigos*,' they confirmed.

'*Por cierto.*'

And she was gone, all backpack and bundled tent.

*

Geronimo remembered the weeks they had spent together, and counted the weeks since Savannah had left. He continued to work in the hotel, to send postcards to his mother and on occasions to sit with Mrs Morgan and enjoy evening chats, almost familial as time went by. Then the postcard arrived from Scotland.

Amigo, I have reached the top! Now I start my return. If you are at number 55 we shall meet again. Savannah X

*

Of course I shall be at number 55! It has become my second home. Friend, friend, friend. Yes, yes, yes. I shall wait, but where are you? No address. No telephone. No contact. A simple spirit drifting south. And dear Mrs Morgan who says: 'If her room is taken in the meantime the occupant will be given an instant notice clause in the terms … when Savannah arrives she shall have back her room.' Dear Mrs

Morgan. Bit like a Mam to me, in a way. And me reciprocating whenever I can. It's company of an evening. I am as contented as I have been for a long while. Well, I do have something to connect me. A kindred spirit, somewhere. A benevolent friendship ... that's what it is with Savannah, and lasting, come what may.

Then tumbled out those troublesome thoughts. The thoughts that cloud contentment like living above the shifting plates that can ignite earthquakes. The what-ifs? If something should befall her, heaven forbid, I may never know. If another dove leads her in another direction. If an extravagance of youthful intrepidness should divert her from number 55, and I never see or hear from her again. Then I shall of have gained much from her friendship, but lost more. When I hint as such to Mrs Morgan she says Savannah is a lovely person, got two feet on the ground, steady ... she'll be back, mark my words. I am a bit of a realist. I must be patient, not to overly concern myself, enjoy just being alive. She has my compass; for sure it will lead her back. When I think of that my heart opens, optimism floods in. I smile. And Mrs Morgan says:

'*Bore da*, Geronimo,' chirpily as she greets me on my way out to work. And away I go, and pass the bench where we had fish and chips. Oh, yes, I have reason to give thanks.

*

Comes the knock. Vanish go the months. Mrs Morgan opens wide her arms.

'Is he still here?'

'Oh *Cariad*, yes.'

Then the big hug—and in go the backpack, the bundled tent and the wide smiles of gratitude. A weight, not heavy but gilded, is lifted at number 55. The kettle is on. Geronimo will return from work a bit later.

'How is he?' asks Savannah.

'Just as you left him. He's a good man.'

*

The three are gathered again. The widow, Geronimo and Savannah. Their daily lives became joined lightly by domesticity, which oiled the heartbeats of a deeper and more silent sentiment. They were like a family quietly looking out for one and other without fuss or word, cerebral in may ways, but giving rise gradually during the weeks and months that followed Savannah's return the suggestion that number 55 had become the spiritual home of the two travellers beneath the umbrella of an empathetic step-matriarch. Always the single-sleepers with their own space riveted in respect and selflessness. The confirmation that a friendship of unfamiliar experience had overcome them during this time set the seal of a lifelong permanency.

Then, one evening, they went downstairs to Mrs Morgan's sanctuary, her parlour. Nothing unusual, but on this occasion they had an announcement to make. They were making preparations to travel.

'Our life is moving on. Although we shall be going our separate ways our hearts will travel together.' Geronimo was explaining to Mrs Morgan the reason, and Savannah was nodding in agreement. They were speaking with one voice, tinged with a sadness that beset the young when decision time rings and the call is best answered. They needed to move on with their lives, to eventually settle.

'Together would be lovely, you two so good with each other,' said Mrs Morgan, clasping her hands on her lap.

'Friends we shall always be, and you Mrs Morgan our first and best we could ever have wished for.' Savannah laid a hand on Mrs Morgan's shoulder confirming a filial fondness that had been born beneath the roof of number 55. 'We have a request. Because we are travelling separately we want a place where we can lodge our addresses, so Geronimo and I will know where the other is, as we move. When we are settled, it will be different, but until then could we send our temporary addresses to you?'

'Like a post box!' Mrs Morgan brightening a little being included, being at the hub of this arrangement. 'Oh, yes. You being such nice guests ... and it will mean I still have contact with you two lovely people. My pleasure, my dears.'

With every intent to keep alive their friendship they packed and set off together retracing their steps, at first, to the old lead mine with its fast food carbuncle, and Mrs G Morgan (widow) giving them a packed lunch—holding back a tear until they were out of sight.

*

Two days later they were camped close to the carbuncle, and enjoying breakfast. The proprietor remembered them, and as if this were a reason he gave extra portions at no extra price knowing they were shortly to set off again. Their gear, packed and ready, rested beside them. The weather was grey

and the lead mine unshaken by activity. Geronimo is study-
ing Savannah.

'Do you have enough money to see you through before
you find work?'

'Yes,' she says. 'And this big breakfast will see me okay
for a day ... or so!' She smiles.

'This is not the end, we shall keep in touch no matter
what. It may be another beginning, another time in our
lives when we go in a different direction, but always we shall
remember the time we spent together ... the pleasure, the
challenges, these moments.' Geronimo laid bare with his
arms the table laden with food. 'Here! Who would have
ever thought that in this wild and desolate yet beautiful
land, you and I have enriched ourselves.' Savannah stretches
out her hand, and Geronimo grasps it, holds it, takes in its
warmth. 'Now is not the time for short-term gifts or prom-
ises ... perhaps it is the time for a long-term gesture in praise
of a friendship we have bestowed with light and benevolence.' All has become quiet. The world has shrunk. The
smell of the fried breakfast filtered away. They are aware
this is a pivotal moment. They are about to part. They may
never see each other again. Geronimo has considered this,
this fear of emptiness, of a loss too valuable to lose and a
friendship of incalculable depth. No gift could replicate its
loss: and he believed it would be a harder loss to bear than
love. Its passion is not physical, not peripheral like love, but
buried deep in the psyche—the come-what-may, I'll always
be there for you. Geronimo opened his wallet and laid a £5
note on the table, smoothed it flat.

'Do you have one of these, Savannah?'

She placed one beside Geronimo's.

'What now, Geronimo?'

'We put our names on these, we tuck them away. They are not for use, save only if we have no money left.'

'Destitute?'

'Not quite. Friendship remains. These are the proof.'

They carefully inscribe their names, and place their £5 notes each in a safe place.

Signatures. Their own writing. Their own moment. They get up, wave farewell to the proprietor and make their way—two separating, departing friends swallowed up amongst the flannel white spots of the landscape.

*

It is about Savannah and Geronimo I remain privileged to conclude testifying about a friendship that spanned all their days with lifelong blessings. Oft unseen yet never forgotten it became a communion of two souls joined by a single thread delicate in its beauty and unbreakable in its evolution. In whatever manner they arranged their lives and in what depth they were taken into other hearts, or took into their own, they never lost contact. They married, raised children, had jobs, changed jobs, enjoyed the privileges of life and suffered the pitfalls of disappointments—and within this choreography their friendship was nourished by knowing whatever their circumstances they would always be there for the other.

Years would pass when they would not see each other, months would vanish without communication. It made no difference because certainty had been woven into the thread binding them together like a double lifejacket keeping their heads above the water of daily difficulties and disappointments that are a part of living. Time, whatever the absences it devoured, enriched their souls. Each with their £5 note, tucked away somewhere, unseen year in year out, but never quite forgotten or unfaded by time. Neither Geronimo nor Savannah became penniless, neither had to fall back upon their note, and the signatures upon them, stayed as fresh as the day fifty years before when they had inscribed them. Then, after all that time, they agreed to frame them. Geronimo hung his on a wall, Savannah placed hers on a mantelpiece. Separate families and separate homes, each a resting place.

Who was she?

Who was he?

A guide to enlightenment. It was the way we were, they would reply.

They would recollect the random white—the shirts in the olive groves and the flannels in the hills before they met, and explain how it was the abiding sense that whatever happened to them was a gift, a unique contribution from a God—or an angel in the form of a pure white dove.

The Dispossessed

Of course, I was much too young to see it like this, the earring that swung from my mother's ear the day she drove me through the gates to the establishment for which I was bound. You see, I sat in the back, a solitary figure watching the swing of the earring at the car's every twist and turn. That's why I remember it so. It dangled like my life. It came to me, not necessarily then, that it was a treasured possession—although it didn't have a new toothbrush like me it was allowed to touch my mother. And laid flat the earring replicated the instant passage from one life to another, from life to fate. Pinched and pierced at the gates the driveway opened pear-shaped, and circuited stonework relentlessly laid, methodical without height or colour, just purposeless flagstones bonded by the gravel drive, which crunched its way in a majestic sweep towards its furthest end before pausing beside an imposing, colonnaded building.

And my mother's earring—is this my lasting memory of her? The piercing, the silver lacework in the shape of a pear, the extravagant dark green emerald at the fall of the drop. The crunch of gravel. The building—the drop. The hushed talk. My suitcase, forlorn. The words unsaid. Worse, the words said that had no depth, shallow words. The smell of change concealed by magicians. And again the crunch of gravel as my mother drove away and distance absorbed her, the earring's reflection swinging to the engine's tune, a solo performer in the rear view mirror.

Then the closing of the heavy doors against possession without.

*

The man said:

'Call me Sir', and indicating the woman who stood back a pace or two from him, 'you call my wife Ma'am. And the man outside … you call him Joe. He carries a rake. There is nothing he does not see. We are a big family here. You will learn other names, learn to help, learn to respect, and learn to learn. How many learns is that?'

'Four.'

'Five! Remember them … there are more to come.'

Sir clapped his hands. Instantly a girl appeared, wearing a blue pinafore, alert. Blue! A colour at last. Bright. Hope. It had a face, subdued, gentle, sorrow deep-set into the eyes.

'Take your case … and follow Rachel.'

Formalities over. The umbrella of comfort unopened.

Empathy up the back stairs somewhere, in the gloom, cowering—perhaps. But blue, nevertheless. Blue replacing the vanishing green of that dark emerald stone. I came to identify the blue as azure, the colour of sky on a clear day so when Rachel wore her blue apron I experienced hope, encouragement not to concede, but to keep my arm above the rising waters pointing to me. When she changed her apron to another colour, those were the bad days.

We had reached a landing. There was a small window that looked out upon the sweep of the drive, the tabled stones, flat, grey, cold—and the gravel that heralded arrivals, and which I was to learn later signalled departures.

'Why does Joe carry a rake?' I asked Rachel.

'Look from the window,' she replied.

So I looked, peeped. There he was, Joe, raking the gravel, obliterating the tread-marks made from the tyres of my mother's car.

Then I felt the first and earliest signs of adult deception—and was awakened to it. That one peep. That one window. Yes, Sir was right, there were other 'learns', and so soon.

'What's your name?' Rachel asked.

'David.'

'No, your other name. David what?'

'David Smyth,' I said.

'You'll be Smyth Two then. There is already another Smyth. He'll become Smyth One. No first names here, well not to begin with. Got to earn those ... like me.'

Further up another flight of stairs and sounds of voices: children's voices, boys' voices—animated, frightening, formidable, clustered. A door half open. Rachel laid a hand on my shoulder, we paused:

'Never cry,' she said.

*

But I did.

The day they took her.

By then, I was blessed. For every blue sky that followed I

thought of her. For every blue sky I felt the warmth of hope. It was of her that I dreamed. Not of my mother, nor of any of my kith and kin of whom I was graciously ignorant, only her. Rachel, courageous Rachel who taught me not to abandon benevolence, to bend with the breeze and to withstand the typhoons. From her I understood deception was not a statutory requirement imbedded into human life. And from her I learned to love, deeply.

I had not been in the institution for very long. For how long had not yet ceased to count, but it was not very long when scratching, digging and desperate to discover any crumbs of sincerity from the wasted containment in which I found myself she came across me sitting on my bed, alone. She stood in front of me, the young warden about her duties, apron blue, weak before Sir and Ma'am—strong before the lesser mortals. I looked up into her eyes and wished she would sit beside me if only for a few seconds. She had kind eyes. There was compassion there, camouflaged. Fear, too, as if other eyes were upon her. Of all the sisters in the world if ever I had had one I would have chosen her, Rachel who called me Smyth Two and who, concealing her soft interior against the barbs of dispossession, stood before me, a quiet presence, a reassurance.

'I love you,' I whispered.

She bent down towards me.

'Love is word we do not use here. It is a dangerous word.'

She was nearest I had ever been to an angel. For her, yes—it was the way she looked at me. Then, at that moment, some unspoken word had passed between us. An understanding is I how best I would describe it.

'I'll teach you to swim … I promise,' she said, before turning and leaving me.

*

Sir and Ma'am were waited on, hand and foot.

Those who served them had first names. Physically blossoming, they were, mentally submissive. They bloomed, and after they bloomed there followed the crunch of gravel, and Joe with his rake. Without trace of coming, or of going, they vanished.

'They were called,' was how Rachel explained it. To be called was an honour as it was an honour to be allowed a first name—stepping-stones to the other side. I thought, when I was told, that the other side would perhaps be my mother, or the house of which I had only faintest memories of early childhood, the house in which I was an obstacle, a mistake, a something that with every year would grow bigger, become more of an obstacle, without value. I wanted to have a first name, but I did not want to be called. I did not remember love in my mother's house. I did not want to be called back there.

Back stairs led to rooms occupied separately by girls and boys. Mixing was not encouraged. Learning together under supervision was as close a contact as allowed. Separated tables at meals. Separated physical activities, separated walks, separated chores, and separated dormitories, ablutions and sick rooms. Clothes passed down. Frugality the watchword. Learn to garden, learn to muck out the animals, learn to eat less and work more. Learn. Learn. Learn.

Learn to be indifferent to those about you.

Learn not affection.

Above all learn to remain silent.

*

During my fourth year there the summer was splendid. The sky seemed to me, as I remembered, a permanent blue. One morning when I was working alone in the glasshouse tending tomato plants Rachel came in. She had blossomed, filled out. No apron of whatever colour could deceive the eye that a young woman stood upright beneath the cotton of her workaday clothes.

Of course, dear Reader, you are wondering what age I may have then been, and maybe what age Rachel had been. For me, thirteen. For Rachel I never knew for sure though I placed her some four years my senior.

'Today I keep my promise,' she said. I must have looked surprised. 'I'm going to teach you to swim, remember?'

'Is that possible?' I asked.

'Sir and Ma'am are away for the day. Go to the swamp after lunch. Be sure Joe does not see you.'

Dispossession, deception, survival—secreted but alive, wriggling beneath the roof of the dark green, graceless building where blue in my eyes was nowhere save on washed aprons and summer skies. The swamp, frighteningly inhospitable and dangerous in the winter when water levels were high and firm ground unexposed. But in the summer ponds of clearer water emerged, and firmer ground surfaced. Whatever the season it was a place strictly out of bounds. Willows, alders, maples exposed trespassers during leafless winters, but during summers they cast shadows, and offered hospitable camouflage. The swamp was a spot where Nature had kept control and sunbeams sometimes danced. Its water rose and fell at its own pace, the levels the gift from the river that bordered the institutional land. Beyond this river a bridge of bolted girders and stone piles carried trains to and from the gilded reaches of fading memory.

After lunch I circumnavigated hopefully away from the eyes of Joe, away from all eyes behind hedge and hill and farmers' crops. I am there, and she was there amongst the willows, apron blue over a swimsuit. She handed me a towel and swimming trunks. The pool was fresh and inviting, the heat given from the sun was warm, a maternal warmth. I changed. She was in the water, standing still, waiting, her top half radiant, and hair auburn about her pale shoulders.

'Come,' she said, opening her arms.

The image. No other image would ever mean so much to me. Oh, how may times I brought it down from my mind when times were dark and distrustful, when life had no tunnels with proverbial lights at their ends. It was as though I had been there, seen the light, had had my due, that I should not complain because many, many others had not been so fortunate.

'Lie on your back, let the water cover you, keep your face above the water, your feet too, if you can. Relax. Breathe in and out, normally. I shall hold you up until you find you are able to float.' Her hands beneath cradled my body, held me so I did not sink: safe hands, hands that touched, hands gentle on my impoverished skin. It seemed no will on my part kept my whole being afloat. I closed my eyes and lay back. Then I believed in angels, and was not dispossessed.

Two further days that summer Sir and Ma'am were away for the day. Two further afternoons I spent with Rachel at the pool, in the swamp. The first on my tummy, her hands on my chest keeping me afloat so I could use my arms and kick with my heels. The second, I reached the other side, unaided. She swam along side me, together. We climbed out and stood on firm ground splashed with the shadows of willows, and striped by the rays of the sun, feral we were and dripping wet. An unfledged boy and a fallow girl, the teacher and the taught.

'Let me see you swim back on your own. I'll watch you from this side,' she said.

Into the water I went and away across to the other side I swam.

Then Rachel followed. I took both her hands and helped her out. I knew I should let go of her hands, but she resisted and we stood close, in silence, committing the sin of the dispossessed—that is being possessed. We were young, our wings had been clipped, but standing wet with exhaustion and weighted by complicity we ascended that free thermal—and I learned of self, and my place in time.

*

Later that summer when the weather was still warm I received the summons. I was required to present myself at Sir's office on a day and at a stated time. I was aware many before had received such summonses, that no rumour needed to be attached. It was a fact of this life.

And Sir was waiting.

'The regulatory arm of this institution is long and reaches far in its need to ensure the well-being of all its parts. It has been brought to my notice that there have been three afternoons when you did not return to your work in the glasshouse. I have recently checked the dates of these afternoons and discover each occurred on days when I was away. Your absence from work is one matter, but your choice of days in which to absent yourself adds a different dimension to the misconduct. Was it because you believed when I am not here my eyes no longer see?'

'No Sir.'

'You expect me, then, to believe each time was coincidental.' Was this a question? I remained silent.

'Have you nothing to say?'

'What is "coincidental"?'

'Coincidental, Smyth Two, means a chance occurrence … that your misconduct was not perpetrated because I was away.'

'It was hot, Sir, in the glasshouse. On those days it must have been hot.'

Sir knew I was putting forward a sort of half-truth. It was the normal air in which we all we breathed, these deceptions being like droplets of life that kept this place going, that nourished it. But I had seen and witnessed the colour of azure blue, and been embraced by it.

'What did you do on the afternoons you absented yourself from work?'

'I walked and found shade, Sir.'

'Where?'

'Along the hedgerows beside the farmer's field. There

61

were rosehips there and cool ditches.'

Sir went to his desk, flicked through papers, every so often glancing at me over the rim of his glasses, owl-like, waiting to swoop.

'Three hours in Room 14? An hour for each misconduct. The punishment will bear down on whether you will be allowed a first name, or not … and thus the date of your calling.' Sir scratched something onto my records, waved the piece of paper at me, dismissing me. Immediately an elder boy came in. He was wearing a clean white shirt, tidy slacks and trainers.

'Room 14, three hours,' he said to the boy.

*

Room 14 was a cell. There were no bars in the window, but the door had a small glass panel that let in vision, but not out. The boy, Daniel, explained this to me so I would know I was being watched. The cell was empty save for a desk and chair, a bucket and a large clock whose white face and blackened hands ticked away time as if it were a pleasurable instrument of torture. It stared at the occupant in the chair knowing it was absolute and beyond restriction. Etched into the desk were the outline of two hands with both thumbs pointing inwards, and for reasons that seemed unnecessary the left hand was marked with an 'L' and the right with an 'R'.

'Smyth Two, you are to sit at the desk and place your hands on the hands marked on the desk. The duration of your punishment is three hours. Move your hands away from the marks and the clock will readjust, and your term will begin as if it had never started. Use the bucket before you sit down.'

The door slammed shut. Silence, save for the ticking of the clock. I walked around the cell, putting off the moment when I would start my punishment. I ignored the bucket. The window, I noticed, was set sufficiently high so that sitting at the desk I might only be able to observe the sky. The chair was solid wood, but it had a back! Not too uncomfortable, I thought. Three hours. I stared at the clock. It stared back at me. I paced about a bit, exercising myself, preparing myself for the long sit. Then I sat down. At once the clock's hands reset themselves at twelve, and the ticking stopped. A red line appeared at the three. One, two, three. Mechanical hours—real, time meaningless. The sooner I start the sooner I finish. I raised my hands above the table, lowered them gently, watched the clock, teased the clock, almost touched the table, but the hands of the clock stayed at twelve. I tried again, even closer to the table this time, but the hands of the clock stayed at twelve. I tried placing only my left hand on the table and as that, too, did not tempt the clock I simply lowered my right hand beside it—then the clock sprang into life, and its cold heart began to beat, its hands twitched almost human in its enthusiasm, and very much at home in this house for the dispossessed.

But for me, not quite—there was Rachel.

On her I focused my mind.

To begin with the hands of the clock appeared deliberately slow. They twitched, but hardly moved across its face. On reflection the first fifteen minutes were the worst because I had not found the way to beat it. Its ticking was mesmeric, slowing real time in my mind, aggravating my senses, and was cruel in its determination to make my three hours not only physically uncomfortable, but to unsettle my brain by tilting its balance against rational thought.

It was the white face—a non-colour, blatant without responsibility against which I eventually closed my eyes and brought Rachel into vision.

Then I felt not alone.

Emboldened.

I allowed my inner self to speak to the clock.

'We share this cell. Should I have occasion to look at you my brain is going to replace your whiteness with azure blue, your whole being with the face of Rachel and your twitching hands with her touching hands. Behind my closed eyes I shall rest content and know I am in a better place, a place untouchable by the ticking of your infamous self.'

And so it was I dreamed, palms resting, at ease: and I let the clock take little satisfaction from its muted ticking.

*

When the cell door was unlocked and I walked free I realised my punishment was easily worth the pleasure of swimming lessons, and that I would willingly subject myself again to that petty rigour (whose diktats enlivened the covert lives of Sir and Ma'am), and abscond again accepting willingly further punishment to swim once more with Rachel.

Rachel.

Is she aware I have been inside Room 14?

Will I ever be able to tell her it was her image that effaced the punishment?

But concealed eyes search, and concealed ears listen.

And all communications were dangerous.

I climbed slowly up the back stairs to the dormitories, thinking about this. When I reached the landing I looked from the window upon the sweep of the drive, the tabled stones, flat, grey, cold. Joe was raking the gravel. My bed had been re-made. It was tidier than when I made it earlier in the day. The dormitory was empty, quiet. Classes and work shifts were still taking place. Tea was a while yet. A corner of a piece of paper poked from beneath my pillow. I must have dislodged the pillow when I sat down because at first I had not seen it. There it was—secreted for a purpose, but to be discovered.

I have been called. Cross the river before you are called.
Swim.
R x

*

How precious is that—that piece of paper? Her writing. Her warning. Her R. Her kiss. And why me?

Then it dawned. I may never see her again. Her blue would remain, as would the sky, but the person that went with it had been called and may have gone—already? Was it her departure Joe was raking? I folded the note, concealed it in the toe of my shoe until I found a safer place. Although it was a dangerous communication it was too precious to be destroyed. It was all I had, all I had ever had of her. It gave meaning to my life, proof that dispossession was not irreversible, that hope existed. However dangerous it was to hold onto that piece of paper I would treasure it, and safe-guard it for all time.

*

The next day I swam.

A bundle of dry clothes lay beside one of the stone piles of the bridge. They fitted a boy of thirteen.

Joe was not called. He was too old—and without value in the market where slaves were sold.

The Walker

… we are at the now.

From within a faded view, and sunk within a pallid face two eyes of cat-like quality peep from behind a curtain of dusty grey material as aged as the face itself—and as dull as its skin wrinkled by timeless time. The eyes take in the boundaries of their focus: that is the two stubborn brick-work columns from which hang heavy gates that are never closed. These structures have become the edges of a stage so that those who pass between them on the other side are the actors who provide entertainment and suggestive imaginations upon which the two eyes glean much pleasure.

The stage has borne witness to the comings and goings of the Shrivenor family—their arrivals and departures, their first embraces and the last farewells. The peeping eyes have witnessed some of this, and history is recorded behind the silent, brooding, wrinkled face—as is the ephemera of daily necessities. Sharp to the minutest detail much inconsequential aspects are tucked away in a brain as small as the head in which it has resided for eighty years, yet as large as the perception of one granted infinite aptitude.

Amelia Regina Shrivenor, spinster is at the now, sitting quietly, watching, waiting to be entertained. It is noontide.

The curtain late risen. The cast is assembling. The village is alert.

*

A group of walkers have gathered in a nearby car park. An aura of intrepidness hangs over them. Determination grits their weathered faces suggesting toil on the land had once been their favoured places of work. This would not be true. It would best to describe them as being from the leisured classes. There may have been about fifteen of them. They flexed their muscles, breathed deeply into their lungs the fresh air and stamped their feet to encourage comfort in their walking boots. They had pencilled into their diaries this first walk of the New Year as soon as the previous autumn had slipped into winter and the walking season for them had ceased. This day, the now day, was an early spring day. It was an inviting and tempting day, fresh and sunny. They had dressed the part, costumed as it were, in shower-proof anoraks, colourful woolly hats and back packs that hung limply from bony shoulders. A few had walking sticks.

There was a leader. A tall, thin ramrod of a man whose hands clutched a map. He was anxious to get started and asserted his authority in a friendly and coaxing manner.

'Five minutes to the off,' he called out.

A lady solid of stature with prominently bandy legs and a woolly hat that came down over her ears had a dog harnessed at the end of a lead. It yapped. It was low-slung and marginally bigger than a cat. It had a red bow tied to a tuft of hair that seemed to sprout for no real reason between its ears. It, too, seemed to be anxious to start.

*

Well, dear Reader, this walking troupe, these unintentional actors strung themselves out into a line and would cross the Shrivenor stage to an already raised curtain and the alerted now-eyes of Amelia Shrivenor. She would blink to clear her eyes, then settle back, and as if touched by world-weariness begin to count the walkers. She would reach the thirteenth, that is the walker behind the lady of stature whose pet is continuing to yap from the sheer excitement of 'walkies at last'—when she pauses, blinks again.

'It couldn't be, surely not!'

*

Let me describe this thirteenth walker, the one whom the cat-like eyes had spotted, and who so aroused Amelia Regina Shrivenor that she leant forward in her seat to obtain a clearer look. The stage is but a short width and he (yes, it was a 'he') soon disappeared off-stage, and was lost to her—gone. He was dressed unlike his fellow walkers. On his head was not a woolly hat but a corn coloured cloth cap whose brim shielded his eyes. He had a light grey jacket zipped from top to bottom, jeans laundered fashion pale and shoes likely to be unsuited for the walk ahead—purple canvas they were with rubber soles. He used a stick in his right hand and on his left wrist below the cuff of his jacket a watch loose on his wrist was partly visible. No pack hung from his shoulders. Amelia Shrivenor's brain had photographed this image. She would revisit it because it titillated her memory. There was more to this man than that, much more. He had a moustache. Bushy grey, manly. He was travelling light, unencumbered, casual as if the walk ahead was no more than going to a corner shop for a paper. He was a little rounded at the shoulders, and leaning forward gave clue to his age that the rest of his image belied. Some would say he was still a handsome man, confident, independent, jovial. Under the peak of his cloth cap there lurked a twinkle.

*

To capture time the year is a helpful peg. Amelia sat playing with her soup and thought about 1962. It was the year after it was found necessary to move from suburbia to the country. Disgraced, they said. The year has lived long in her memory because it was the year she became a woman—that is she left behind maidenhood and entered the adult world. She had transcended the conceived barriers that had punctuated her life at boarding school, which her parents believed to be an acceptable depository where Amelia could obtain an education suited to their aspiration for her. Simply, this aspiration was a good marriage. Decorum and deportment, domestic science and physical activity, music lessons and drama, skirts primed to just below the knee—walking in threes! For sure, unsullied by the brutal world of boys! Of men, they maintained, she would discover through a good marriage.

In 1962 Amelia Regina met Albert Augustus. She was nineteen and without blemish. He was twenty-two and apparently a man of the world.

Amelia was excessively pretty. Stirring boys had ogled her, but by 1962 men had taken more than a serious interest in her, being quite persistent. She was petite, obscured and lived at home. Men called and went. One or two were suitable. Her parents waited. Then Albert Augustus arrived; from where no one was quite sure. He was handsome, well possessed—and if anything was left from his boyhood it had been erased by National Service. Albert was a man sure of himself, seemingly affluent, charmingly casual, gracious to Amelia's parents—patient. He had a car whose roof folded back. By the summer of that year there was an acceptance that betrothal was on the cards, but nothing definite. Hushed tones pervaded the house when he was there, the house on high alert, champagne standing by to be cooled. The once rigorous rules that tethered Amelia were relaxed. If she came in late little mention of it was made save an acknowledgement that 'it had been noted'. Did she have a nice time? Where did they go? Questions not pursued for exactitudes, but only for loose generalities. Veiled questions, searching maybe, but never disturbing the water.

*

Amelia was besotted. Most weekends she and Albert would drive somewhere. To the coast, to a pub, to a film. They hugged and canoodled in the car—top open in fine weather: top down in inclement. They called the car Tulip. Whenever her parents questioned her it was always: Tulip took us there or Tulip went the long route or Tulip loves the dunes— like Tulip was the companionable chauffeur to whom they always deferred. In late October Tulip took them to meet two of her old school girl friends. Amelia's pride in Albert was prodigious. They would meet her friends at a small music festival to be held in a farmer's field off the beaten track. They would take a train from where they would walk the remainder of the way carrying tent and provisions. For Amelia this was an adventure, life was opening wide, really wide, and her whole self exploding in a delight at discovering intrepidness at a 'street' level she never knew existed. This freedom to breathe without question, this loose activity where life followed a natural and unimpeded furrow lit only by the promise of something marvellous, unseen but awaiting around a distant corner. Albert was fun loving, gallant and praised her beauty.

The day they tramped along the track to the festival Amelia said:

'You are a real gentleman.'

'And you, my best-beloved, are "just so"?'

'In what way am I "just so?"'

'Because you are just so unlike a dalmation.' Albert smiled.

'In what way,' she teased.

'You are spotless ... and how you were made spotless I shall tell you.' She stretched up as they were walking and kissed his cheek. 'Because you were bathed in charcoal soap!'

The festival site was dotted with colourful little tents, the occasional derelict caravan and the fanciful painted vans flaunting unroad-worthiness. Guitarists, many cross-legged and independent, wafted mournful music across the site. Scattered folk wandered without haste, without recourse to

72

time. A feeling of relaxation away from an anxiously busy world was what struck Amelia. Individual independence pervaded beneath an umbrella of tribal cohesion. Friendliness was paramount, problems shared—this loosely knitted family struck her as a beautifully structured experience as she watched Albert pitch their tent. The gaily dressed young people wore clothing tuned to reflect their personality. For the recently released Amelia from the controlling influence of her parents the scene unfolding before her seemed unreal—and she an observer of an unfolding fable. Later she would learn the smoking of 'grass' was a pastime rich in custom and not the veiled, notorious and unacceptable persuasion that fashioned the rigours of her upbringing.

Albert spread the rug outside the tent.

They sat down.

Folk passed, slowed for the pleasantries of the day. Many of these folk Albert had met before because they exchanged Christian names with the familiarity of the reasonably well acquainted.

Amelia's school girl friends arrived. Hand-in-hand they were, and comfortably at home in the surroundings. Carrying a tent and spurred like 'troopers' they were organised, good-natured, were a neat and precise couple, emotionally close and compact. Albert made coffees, and all four formed a loose, sitting circle. Upon them formed a serene and angelic ambience, and Amelia's real world floated away leaving unfettered the blooms of a different life. She breathed in deeply the rural air, and gazed at Albert as a devotee gazes upon an icon—believing in him all was possible.

*

The stars came out, slowly one at a time. The ground released its warmth into the evening atmosphere. The murmuring guitars became distant, and inside the tent a descending shadow fell. The quiet and determined gentleness of sex was what Amelia would remember. The advent into womanhood so beautifully engineered transcended any fear of the unknown.

'Oh! Yes, yes,' she thought. 'The same for most women … but impossible to be so beautiful.'

'Thank you, thank you, thank you.' Her words drifted out—yet failed to reach Albert. He was asleep.

In the next tent she listened to the suppressed, cloistered whispers of her two friends, and she sighed her own long, impassioned sigh of a love bestowed and to be garnered for all time.

The next day the rains came washing away all majesty of the festival. Boggy ground, motors reluctant to start, the sound of wheels spinning with out grip, the field slowly emptying. Its festival goers plodded sodden towards the railway station—she, Albert and her two friends amongst the dejected surge. She remembered that walk through the rain with her friends and Albert robust, laden with gear, strong, resolute, manly, the man she had given herself to—more, her man and she his best-beloved.

But she would not see him again.

She waited, pined and quietly wept.

Eventually she dried her eyes and faced the world again.

*

… we are at the now again.

Amelia Regina Shrivenor is waiting for the curtain to rise before the final act. It is teatime. The cast is returning, spread out, foot sore and weary. The leader is proudly leading his troupe, and beside him the lady of stolid stature and yapping dog.

*

Dear Reader, we have jumped a lifetime. The mists that once shrouded 1962 have lifted—just for a while. Memories long buried but not forgotten have been raised above the detritus of human disregard, and Amelia has steeled herself. She waits serenely, as is the prerogative of old age, for the walking troupe to reappear across her stage. She has hung from a brickwork column, which hold one of the heavy gates, a notice. This notice, though hastily inscribed, cannot be missed:

If you are Albert who had a car called Tulip please knock.

Amelia, somewhat pleased with her powers of observation and astuteness, stirred her tea, absorbed the aroma that straddled the porcelain of her cup of China tea and let the expectation of a challenge course through the bones of her ageing body. This day was going to be different. It may have been long in the coming, but the wait had all the prospects of a deserving drama!

Across the stage they came—the leader, the lady, and the yapping dog. Unbeaten by the trek followed the woolly hats, the walking sticks, the flat back packs that clung to bony shoulders, and the genial smiles of relief of the beneficial exercise successfully accomplished. Amelia adjusted her glasses, blinked to clear her watery eyes, leant forward, and focused her whole self so as not to miss a single second if the trap she had cunningly set—was sprung.

Spread out they came! Amelia judged most had crossed the stage before the few stragglers came on—wearied but not defeated. Amongst them, casually ambling and seemingly untroubled, came the man with the corn coloured cap. As he approached the brick column he shortened his paces before halting beside the notice to read it more carefully. Amelia, peeping from behind her curtains, watched him scratch the back of his neck—his face dedicated to bewilderment. Her man, she was convinced he was her man, took an interest in the wristwatch that hung loosely from his wrist as though time had become significant.

'Sign of nerves!' exclaimed Amelia to herself.

Her man, now alone whence the stragglers had gone, stood still in contemplation before moving centre stage and shrugging his shoulders in a nonchalant manner as if confronting a coincidence. He gazed at the house with its portico entrance and at the regal maroon-painted front door with its impressive brass knocker, which drooped in solemn anticipation.

'Got you!' Amelia, tap-tapping the porcelain rim of the teacup, smiled the wily, self-congratulatory smile of a rejected woman about to harvest retribution.

Up the short drive he came with a confident gait borne on assured shoulders characteristic of a man whose experiences included handling the unexpected. He sensed unseen eyes followed his every pace, twitch and pause—and even his every thought! This sense urged him to display an image of superiority, which would imply a confrontational ability, should it be necessary, to ride out difficulty or diversion.

His bearing, thus, suggested to Amelia life had most probably been good to him.

He gave the knocker a robust knock, knock, knock.

A maid, pinafored and with discrete demeanour, opened the door and showed him in. The hall was cool, carpeted Indian style and set about with ancestral furniture. A grand-father clock chimed the hours of four.

'Time,' thought Albert, 'what trick is it about to play?'

Close to the clock nestled a door of polished oak the other side of which was the drawing room where Amelia sat poised and primed. There was quietness as though church mice lived there—a lurking awareness there was life, a place perhaps of little feet and sensitive whiskers!

The maid tapped reverentially the door and announced:

'Your visitor, ma'am.'

Your … I am expected then! Albert smiled, took a deep breath, gripped his walking stick and crossed the thresh-old. He noted the elegant soft furnishings of pale blues and greys, the silver framed photographs and porcelain figurines on the mantelpiece, the cut flowers in the grate beneath—then the lady tucked away who sat imperiously on the right, by the window, her face held back without expression. He turned towards her, and with courtly respect doffed his corn coloured cap.

'It is Amelia, isn't it?' Then bending low in exaggerated homage he added: 'Of course it is! And you're looking so well.'

'Sit down, Albert. It has been a long time.'

She scrutinised his face through partly closed eyes, and adjusting her focus wheeled back time and memory, and the swathes of life that had passed since she last set eyes on him. In silence she stared at this man now sitting at her table, the empty cup waiting to be filled—and time itself suspended between the *now* and the *then* to be erased by humiliation or forgiveness.

'Here you are now ... and still a walker! Remember the time we walked to the festival.' Amelia's face gave hint of a steely smile laced gently with the cunning of one holding a good hand of cards. Albert knew he was caught. How clever she was to mention that walk. They had walked, their last day together, when they had made love in the tent and walked back in the rain all those years ago. She had, without mentioning it, brought to the surface the Achilles's heel of their estrangement. And now an empty cup waited, which Albert discerned could be a symbol of a peace offering.

'I couldn't be sure it was you when you passed, but my body sensed, triggered a mental reflex, awoke the aspirational dust of a time not yet removed in deep sleep. I had not quite abandoned thoughts what may have come of you. Then you passed my door! How many years on? I can tell you ... sixty years on! I do not wish to know how you filled those sixty years, nor do I wish you to ask me how I filled those years. But, Albert, I see in you the residue of an independent spirit.'

'And, Amelia, I see in you the sparkle of our earlier encounters.' He lowered his head deferentially.

'Sparkle ... that was extinguished when you forsook

me! Nevertheless, time has brought us face to face again by the flickering chance as you passed my gates. Life can play tricks, and it seems to me, Albert, it is the completion of a circle when time has almost dulled memories leaving them lurking on the cusp of extinction. Memories of the day at the festival hung like a weight around my neck although its heaviness diminished as the years slipped by allowing its burden to become tolerable.'

'I should have told you, tried to explain, but I was not strong enough to witness the hurt in your face and the tears in your eyes if I had done so. We had great fun together, experiencing fondness and how to delight each other ... but we were novices trespassing on life's learning curve.'

'I did not feel it then as trespass. You led me to believe togetherness and ... dare I say, love was in the offering. It seemed, reflecting afterwards, you led me along a false trail towards some holy grail favoured by you.'

'I saw benefits for both of us.'

'Different benefits?'

'Yes, different benefits because we were concerned with the daily practicalities that affected us separately.'

'Dear Albert, surely you are not telling me our trip to the festival was forged behind the buttress of pragmatism!'

'I am simply trying to say we were young and lived in some way under the umbrella of our families. We were not entirely free whilst being enticed into adulthood.'

'Enticed! You were already an adult ... and I was not! You took me to the brink, dangled me over it, then let me drop exploited and discarded. You stole from me that which can never be returned. And now you are at my table posturing. I collected myself from where you dumped me, picked myself up, cleaned myself down from what was beautiful to what became dirty ... carried alone the indignity of being lasciviously sullied.'

This went home. Amelia could see, almost felt for Albert as he was taken aback by this verbal onset, and as if to suggest a hint of clemency when there would be none she hovered the teapot above the empty cup.

'I'm sure you must need some tea after your walk.' And not waiting for an answer: Milk? Sugar? 'I do not wish to dwell on that day sixty years ago ... it has now long gone, but I am confident you would not want any daughter of yours to have been put in the position in which you put me.' She began to pour, then passed over the cup poised as it was on its delicate saucer her face expressing the calm satisfaction that awaits the certainty of success—and a moment of retribution long in the waiting.

'I cannot say ... I have no children.'

A steely silence settled—a pause liken to an entrapped mouse knowing the slightest move will cause the cat to pounce. Albert didn't cower, only did the knots of ambivalence tighten in his brain disturbing his focus on a gentlemanly exit. He sampled the tea carefully returning the cup to its saucer, and for a second or two wondered if this unexpected encounter, which could have brought pleasure, would outweigh the feelings of entrapment. Oh, yes! He looked at Amelia and discerned she had aged with dignity, and he ventured she had discovered the nobility of ageing. This consideration, though fleeting, set in motion a wave of regret that distracted the time-worn memories of the recklessness of aspiring adulthood.

Amelia Regina rang a tiny silver bell.

The maid appeared.

'Please show the visitor out.'

Albert Augustus, startled at Amelia's brusqueness, shifted uncomfortably in his chair. She gazed at him—and the storm clouds of the yesteryears began again to overwhelm her.

'We could have cried together,' she sighed.

'I don't understand,' he said.

Amelia shrugged. The maid held open the door and waited respectfully. Albert stood up, and feeling measurably enfeebled clutched firmly his walking stick.

'You had a daughter,' Amelia fired at him.

Albert glanced back at her.

'Did you say *had* or *have*'?

'Had,' she replied.

Pepita's Bridge

Gabriella believed the little bridge was more than a crossing place between her home and the world beyond. She dreamed about it. And the dream recurred, unlike other dreams that passed away during a single, delusional moment. The bridge was real, it existed beyond the front gate of the cottage, and all that happened in its orbit was part of her life of which she was bound to conform, and to be a part of the life she witnessed when she was awake. Within all the memories of this bridge stood her grandmother. '*Stood*' was the word she used when she wished to describe her Nannan because her Nannan stood tall in physique and virtue. She epitomised the strong, tenacious, country woman brought up in peasant hardship, widowed from misfortune at an early age and for reasons not clearly elucidated brought up her granddaughter as her own child.

The bridge was made of wood and was patched with repairs. It was sturdy enough to carry the essentials for human life, but not a horse with a cart. A horse on its own was probably its limit. Into one of the midway timbers of the bridge two initials had been carved. They were worn with age, and lichen encrusted.

On a day, in the eighth year of her life, Gabriella took

a small brush and scrubbed clean the initials. Thereafter she would run a hand over them whenever she crossed the bridge. Beneath the bridge a stream of clear water rumbled and tumbled over stones and rural debris, and through the reeds that clung to its banks. In the winter months it raged and mouthed and strove to spread its burden over its banks; but in the summer months it ran lucid and cool, spreading a gentle, rippling sound—a time beloved by Gabriella who bare-footed its waters.

It was a tranquil place, unvisited—an idyll.

And Gabriella? To the outside world she did not exist. She had arrived from a place unknown. She had not even become the most inconspicuous dot on any demographic survey. She had, in all intents and purposes, save for her Nannan, left no footprints.

*

Once a week, most weeks, Nannan would take Gabriella into town. Usually on market day, they would cross the bridge together and walk the fifty or so yards to the disused barn where the old Ford was kept. There were occasions when Nannan would go alone. Then it was:

'Gabriella, I would like you to stay at home today. I have business to attend to, and you would be bored. You can walk with me to the car, if you like.'

One such a day in May, before the millennium turned, when the world appeared fresh, alive, expansive and when all things suggested joyousness to the wide-eyed Gabriella who had developed an adventurist and questioning nature. She had reached her tenth birthday. The sun shone, the stream glinted and the harmony of country summer filled the air. Nannan had driven off. The old Ford offered its usual backfiring and expunged oil farewell as Gabriella began to retrace her steps towards the cottage. A man was standing on the bridge. He had appeared from nowhere, as if he had waited hidden until the old Ford had driven away. She had spotted him and knew he had spotted her. She slowed her pace. The man waited, made no move to come towards her. Quite still he was, frightening without movement or sound—like a shop's dummy, she thought. He had a camera that hung from his neck. When she was nearer to the bridge he raised his camera, placed it attentively to his right eye, and photographed her, not once but several times in succession, quickly, professionally. Gabriella continued to walk slowly towards the bridge. The man hung his camera back on his shoulder, and watched her as she approached. She was cautiously unafraid, and the man had not moved since he had re-slung his camera. Indeed, she had reached the end of the bridge before the man fluttered a hand in acknowledgement of her presence.

'If you wanted to see my Nannan you have just missed her,' said Gabriella.

'It is of no matter,' said the man.

'For a *no matter* you have come a long way,' said Gabriella. The man raised his eyebrows confirming to himself the young girl who stood but ten childlike paces before him had a delightful manner of expression—adult for her age, but innocent.

For Gabriella to reach her cottage she would have to cross the bridge and pass close to this man, although he was not blocking her way, only did it appear to her that he was. She took off her shoes, tucked the hem of her long, linen skirt into her knickers and carrying her shoes waded across the stream to emerge at its other side. She replaced her shoes, unhooked the hem of her skirt, swept back from before her face long tresses of dark, unbrushed hair, cocked her head to one side, put her back to the man on the bridge and walked earnestly with her back towards him along the path that led to the cottage.

'Spirited,' the man said to himself in a voice that carried no distance, but was meant to be heard.

For her part Gabriella did what many young girls would have done. She closed firmly the cottage door behind her, and went at once to an upstairs window with a good view of the bridge, and peeped unseen.

The man? Well, he had done what he was paid to do. And he had raised his camera again to take a succession of shots at Gabriella's retreating, determined, almost coquettish strides towards the cottage.

'Spirited,' he had said to himself again, before setting off down the track between the hedgerows, and disappearing from Gabriella's view.

*

A week later the letter from Cardiff arrived. Typed on vellum laid paper, with an embossed logo.

Dear Mrs Llewellyn,
It is regarding Gabriella, your granddaughter that I write
on behalf of Creative Artistes. We have been instructed by

a well-respected impresario to find a girl of about ten years of age to play a leading role in a stage play. Our instructions are, briefly, that the girl is petite, has dark hair, is of a spirited and unconventional temperament, is naturally comfortable in an environment that lacks modern pursuits, and that the most suitable girl for the part would be one whose upbringing has been constrained by orphanhood.

I enclose a stamped and addressed envelope for your response. I can assure, Madam, in matters of legality and welfare, our good selves will cover all expenses involved in the selection for the part.

Yours sincerely
Hugh Jenkins

*

The letter was a godsend to Mrs Llewellyn. Though not a churchgoer since she believed God had struck down her husband in his prime for no other reason that he was carrying a flagon of ale on a Sunday when the lightening bolt found him beneath an oak. Gabriella, from a different perspective, believed Cardiff to be brick-wicked, dark and shadowy, bridgeless, without streams or tracks or woodland clearings. Her God, if she had one, was in and around the bridge—just the other side of the garden gate. At the time of the letter's arrival she was still inclined to believe the swans, whose nest was up stream amongst the reeds, were angels in disguise sent to her as companions. So it was when Nannan said the letter was a godsend, Gabriella wondered if it could be, indeed that the swans were but the messengers—witnesses, vestal white, serene, faithful and beautiful.

With wings, too!

'Could these people not come here and see me?' asked Gabriella.

'I do not expect so, dear. Auditions take place in bright lit rooms with cameras and voice recording machines.'

'I have seen pictures of Cardiff, Nannan. It looks inhospitable.'

'To those who live in Cardiff where you live would seem inhospitable.'

'Who would know I live here?'

'That I cannot say.'

'Is that, Nannan, because you do not know, or that you do know but cannot say?'

'My dear, you are such a lovely child, but quite sharp for your age!'

'It is you ... and the swans who have taught me to be sharp.'

'So, Gabriella, what have you learned from me and the swans?'

'To serve ... and to keep my own company.'

'Goodness me! To serve! That was not my intention.'

'I think I shall see it as a blessing.'

With that Nannan placed a gentle kiss on Gabriella's forehead and said:

'My dear Gabriella ... it is you who are my blessing.'

*

It was a summer's day in July when the car came to take them to Cardiff. It was all shiny and black, and looked out of place as it waited on the far side of the bridge. The driver was very polite; opening the door for them, explaining how they could open and close the windows, control the temperature—and how they could listen to the radio. And where there were sweets suitable for travellers, and water. There was a deep smell, forced. Nannan was uncertain if it was a healthy smell like the smell of hay and dung and all things earthy. The driver assured her.

'Purifies with fragrance, Madam,' he said.

'Leathery,' said Gabriella.

*

Dear Reader, we need to glimpse this young girl. There is an immediate sense she is moulded by Nature with unspoilt and unpolished features beneath the abundance of dark hair that falls to her shoulders. Her skin is gently bronzed to an ochre blush, which indicates a complexion garnered from outdoor pursuits. Her comportment is modest and retiring, yet her gaze is alert. She is alive, vital, crouched like a kitten about to spring. She has the aura of an angel—with the suggestion of indignancy aspiring to a more rare beauty. The light shines on her. This day she is dressed with deference for the occasion, yet subtly. Her skirt is three-quarters in length, made from cotton, colourful, wide-hemmed. She has on a white, loose, blouse with floral embroidery around its top over which she has gathered an orange scarf light in weight that hangs about her shoulders. She is wearing a pair of neat 'pixie' boots quite unsuited for the countryside.

*

Cardiff: street upon street. In Gabriella's eyes the surrounding walls of its medieval castle dominate. Behind these walls the octagonal tower is perched like a stook with the flagged red dragon hoisted on a pole. City life—alive with the bustle of busy people with no obtrusive aim, and whose clamour of selfish discord sitting disgruntled amidst the waft of gasoline fumes. Nannan remembers. Gabriella, in defence of the rurality in which she has been brought up, closed her eyes at sights she perceived to be obscene. The unhoused beggars with tethered dogs in doorways of over-stocked shops, the poverty of dress, the enforced waddle of the overweight, the massed discipline of people organised to move (or not to move) by the colour of a light.

'How do people find their homes? How do they ever get back to where they came from?' she asked Nannan.

'They have maps and buses.'

'But no stars. And no tracks or special trees. No field gates. No single lights from single cottages at night.'

'They navigate, only it is different from the way we do at home.'

The car pulled up. Steps. Polished brass railings to an automatic door. Reception desk, and the keen sense of business and efficiency. A polite and powdered receptionist smiled, welcomed them, and enquired about their journey. At a glance she took in Gabriella—saw the outward qualities, and why she was selected for audition.

'You must be Gabriella.'

Gabriella rather sweetly lowered her head in majestic obeisance.

'Yes, I am her.'

And the receptionist gave Nannan one of those open,

understanding looks that convey pleasure at their meeting. Then, with a tilt of the head she raised eyebrows and glanced again at Gabriella to indicate to Nannan she can be justly proud of her exquisite granddaughter.

The driver said he was at their disposal. Whenever they were ready he would take them home.

*

The director of the play is very cordial. He has taken them to his office and offered them refreshment. Just the three of them, save for a secretary discreetly placed in one corner. He is examining, in a fatherly and discreet manner, Gabriella. He narrows his eyes, taps upon the top of his desk the rubber end of a pencil. The word *sublime* crosses his mind. Then he directs his attention to Nannan, the guardian of this thought-provoking child.

'I am to direct a play at the Wales Millennium Centre, hopefully in the autumn. The play is set in South America during the eighteenth century. The central character is the eponymous Pepita who is an orphan under the care of an abbess. Pepita has been taught to serve and to obey within the orphanage, and has tuned her worth to become unselfish and menial. I have to say the part will not be an easy one, but I have come to the conclusion if I can find a girl whose experience of orphanhood is real, and whose childhood has not been cemented by modern habits then the role will flow more easily … will be unforced and natural. It has to shine, to dominate the stage. It is a part for a girl whose nature has not been hampered by the transient environment of today. The part has to be lived as though for real, and to be experienced by audiences as for real. I have to say, Nannan, there is stardom to be acclaimed, yet it would be inappropriate if stardom were allowed to settle on the shoulders of your granddaughter. I shall accept tears, but not universal acclaim.'

'Why tears?' asked Nannan musingly. Her face reflected worldly wisdom, cut by furrowed wrinkles and wise eyes that had experienced many seasons.

'There are tears of joy and there are tears of sadness. It is not possible to say which it will be when a story is beautiful.'

Nannan smiled. She liked this man. She smiled a kindly and encouraging smile to Gabriella who, with the gentlest flicker of her eyelashes, acknowledged that her grandmother was satisfied with how things were going.

*

Gabriella was placed amidst the tumult of lights, cameras and recorders—and persons armed with clipboards, fast moving pencils and mobile phones. They would probe her physical presence and emotional psyche to establish if they met the requirements for the leading part—and whether audiences would find in her an exhilarating performer. The air in the studios was stuffy with powerful lights and recording instruments pumping invisible heat into confined areas. Politeness and concern helped to mitigate discomfort, but money was at stake, and a fever requiring exactitude and penetration into the decision-making process, which was concealed as best as could be from her. Time, on occasions, seemed in short supply.

Thus it was with relief when the black and shiny car pulled up beside the little bridge leading to her cottage, and the car door was opened—and she and Nannan got out breathing a sigh of relief. Gabriella, as was her custom, ran her fingers over the carved initials on the bridge. Her grandmother noticed. Two swans watched their arrival. Gabriella smiled to them, waved a gentle hand. She was home. Her angels were there, and so was the bridge.

*

The next day.

'Nannan, why is it I am not told who those initials belong to?'

'You have not asked. Only do you find comfort from them.'

'Nannan, the swans know, don't they?'

'Gabriella … they could. They do live for twenty to thirty years.'

'My swans live forever.'

'That cannot be.'

'Yes, Nannan. They are angels, they live forever.'

'For you, dear Gabriella, they will live forever. But they will not live forever for everyone.'

Gabriella went to the window. The bridge. The swans. The initials. A quiet loneliness existed in Gabriella's heart. Was it loneliness, experienced—or love inexperienced? There was this something at times like this when life seemed safe and wonderful and full. Then there were the other times when life seemed unsafe and indifferent and empty—like yesterday. But just then, this day after yesterday, the thought occurred to her, as it had done before. What would it be like to have had a brother or a sister—someone with whom to share a secret place, to share a secret thought and to share a secret thing?

'Those initials?' I shall ask the swans, thought Gabriella.

But the swans were not at the bridge when Gabriella went to ask. She knew they would not be far, but she needed to point to the initials. And the bridge was the place to read the minds of angels. For two days the swans were not to be seen at the bridge, and those days were empty days for Gabriella.

'Nannan, there have been no swans at the bridge for two days and I wanted to ask them about the initials.'

'Dear Gabriella, sit with me for a while. In the garden, somewhere in the shade. Bring a cool drink, and a straw.'

So they sat, grandmother and granddaughter. Close they were, and at ease with each other. Blessed. The bridge stretched silent above the limpid flow. Only the distant sounds of a labouring tractor, and the bleating of a lamb crying for its mother came to them.

'They are the initials of your father and mother. Your father carved them when he was not much older than you. He and his playmate loved the bridge. It was their playground, and where they learned to love one and other as they grew older. Bleddyn, your father, was my son, and Liliwen his dear, dear lifelong friend lived in a cottage that no longer exists. It had to go ... to make a new road. Bleddyn was a man at an early age, and Liliwen was beautiful like you. You are her image. They, too, loved the swans. They would play with them. They gave them names. I think they almost tamed them. They all shared the water beneath the bridge.' Nannan placed a comforting hand on Gabriella's shoulder. The memory of those days easily brought tears to her eyes. There are tears of joy and tears of sadness. Yes, the director of the play was right. Gabriella sat still as her grandmother struggled to open silent memories that had once harnessed so much love and hope—and then so much grief.

'Liliwen, is a very pretty name,' said Gabriella.

'It did suit her. White as a lily she was … white as a swan. Maybe I shouldn't say this, but it was a beautiful sight to see Bleddyn and Liliwen naked in the water, when they were much younger that is, naked with the swans. They were all so white, and about the same size!' Nannan smiled at the memory, then wiped away a tear. A long period of silence. Time for heartache to settle, to take in fresh breaths ready for more unharnessed memories to come.

'Your father and mother drowned. They passed away together … it was how they would have wanted to go, holding on to each other not wanting to be left behind. In the *llyn (pool)*. Swimming they were. Hot summer's day. Cold water. An accident. It was said your mother got into difficulties and your father tried to save her.'

'How old was I?'

'You were three. You were their gift to the world.'

And they went back into the cottage and comforted each other. In the fragile peace more words came.

'They are buried side-by-side in the Llanfair churchyard. Shall we go and visit them one day?' suggested Nannan.

Gabriella thought.

'I do not think they will be there.'

'Why is that, dearest?'

'God has changed them into swans and sent them back to me as angels.'

'You were so young.' And Nannan shook her head and wept copiously.

*

Not long afterwards the letter came, from the director. It was personal, assuring, gave confidence. It expressed delight, and explained to Nannan that Gabriella has been chosen to play the part. There will be a need for a stand-in, eventually. It would be best if Gabriella stayed in a house in Cardiff, which was used by the producers of plays for their actors. Attendance at school would be arranged, if necessary. Nannan would be welcome to stay in the facility whenever she wished. The necessary contract would be arranged if Gabriella accepted the part. He hoped very much she would, as it seems it was made for her. Nannan was to contact him direct if she has any worries at all. It was a big decision for both of them, and he readily understood.

The name of the play is Pepita's Bridge. There will be some early exposure in the media of its opening.

An early reply would be appreciated.

*

So it was Nannan and Gabriella set off one afternoon in September for Cardiff in the shiny, black car. They locked up the cottage, crossed the bridge, acknowledged the driver who took their small suitcase—and seated themselves comfortably for the ride.

'Your father and mother would be proud if they could see you now,' said Nannan laying a hand on Gabriella's arm.

'I shall do my best for them, Nannan, and I shall do my best for you.'

'You are unspoilt. It is my wish you remain so. It would be your father's and mother's wish also. Even when you are under the spot light the director wants you to be your natural self. Be modest. Take applause with lowered head and lowered eyelids. You are to play the orphan that you are. Sometimes it is prudent to walk in the shadows, to walk behind and not in front, to listen and not to speak save only to smile upon the talker. Remember the little plot of ground where you were raised, where you are treasured, and we both were blessed. Your angels are there, beneath the bridge, whenever you return. They are constant, they have memories, they are faithful just as your father and mother were faithful to each other.' The car ran smoothly towards Cardiff.

'Nannan, tell me about the Pepita I am to play. I know she is taken from a book, and the book tells the lives of those who died when the rope bridge they were crossing broke. Why an orphan? What is special about an orphan?'

'The five who died when the bridge broke were all special. And the orphan no more or less so. What they had in common was an involvement with love. Pepita was an orphan who had grown up in a convent. She was taught to be obedient and faithful. She was sent to be a maid of a rich woman whose own daughter had deserted her. Pepita is lonely and unhappy, and feels neglected. She is still only a child. Pepita inspires the rich lady to write a letter of love to her daughter. Two days later Pepita and her mistress died when the bridge broke.'

'Why would a daughter desert her mother?'

'Maybe the mother was rich and gave her daughter only little attention.'

'Were Pepita and the rich lady blessed like you and I?'

'We are family. I expect they lived together in a different way. I know you are lonely, and unhappy at times, though you do not often show it. I have tried not to neglect you.'

'I love you Nannan, but I am afraid.'

'But why?' Nannan put her arms around Gabriella and drew her to her.

'The bridge on the stage will not be our bridge,' said Gabriella.

'Because our bridge is real.'

They were approaching Cardiff. Nannan and Gabriella had fallen silent. Nannan, wishing to replace the ferment of anxiety, had an idea.

'Shall we find you a playmate ... a boy, free and adventurous like your father when he was a boy? Maybe an orphan, and give him a home.'

'Where do we find such a boy?'

'Why! Here in Cardiff. I shall make enquiries, and you may find one playing the part of an orphan on the stage ... playing an extra!'

'I should like that, Nannan. We could take him home with us ... when the play has finished.'

'These things take time. They do take time. We can

97

only do our best.'

Gabriella smiled.

'Then that is what we shall do,' said she fervently.

*

Pepita's Bridge ran for a month. Its last performance was at the end of October. The reviews were good:

Pepita's Bridge is a play adapted from Thornton Wilder's book, The Bridge of San Luis Rey, and is set in Peru in the eighteenth century. Its eponymous orphan, Pepita, is under the care of the Abbess of the convent who finds her a place as a servant to the Marquesa, who is rich, difficult in character and self-centred, and whose daughter has deserted her. Pepita has been groomed to obey and serve, and to begin with the Marquesa takes little notice of her. In time she does notice her, recognises her selflessness and wishes a daughter like her. Learning from Pepita's qualities the Marquesa writes an impassioned letter to her daughter seeking forgiveness.

Two days later the Marquesa and Pepita are crossing an Inca rope bridge, which has existed for a hundred years, when it snaps. They are amongst the five victims on the bridge who fall to their deaths in the river below. A Franciscan monk, who witnesses the disaster, seeks to find a theological reason why it is these five who are destined to perish.

Gabriella is the star of this play—a rising one if she continues a career on the stage. What is delightful is her unforced portrayal of the orphan child who grows in maturity, yet loses none of her quiet modesty and selflessness. She is beautifully cast, and gives a dazzling performance. The direction of the play is majestic. A real triumph.

*

Nannan had noticed the boy playing the part of Don Jaime.

A sickly boy, and not quite an orphan in the play! Though he, too, fell to his death when the bridge snapped his part was not an influence on the main story line. He was characterised to have seizures (credited to his father's poor health), to be sensitive and sublime. His mother was an actress and his mother's mentor had in some manner, brought him up. On stage he had played this part with commitment, and engendered amongst the audience tugs at their heartstrings.

Off stage he was a total orphan, under social care. Rhys by name.

He had the prospect of becoming a strikingly handsome young man. He was of Gabriella's age. Nannan watched him carefully. They had early suppers together, and teas when there was a matinée—often just the three of them. Nannan would not have been human if she had not found a resemblance, indeed sought one, between Gabriella and Rhys—and Liliwen and Bleddyn. Gabriella and Rhys did chat together, became companionable during the stresses of learning their parts and playing to admiring audiences.

'What is it like being in care?' asked Gabriella.

'Caged,' said Rhys.

'What you mean, caged?'

'You know, not free. Too many rules.'

'What sort of rules?'

'You know ... times to wake up, times to go to bed,

times to eat, times to go out, times to go in.'

'They only looking after you and keeping you safe. If you had a mother and a father they would use the same rules, wouldn't they?'

'I suppose. Does your Nannan have rules?'

'Oh, yes, Rhys, she does.'

Silence then.

'I bet she doesn't lock all the doors so you can't escape!'

'We have two doors ... one front and one back. She does lock them at night. Not to keep me in. Keep bad people out.'

'Do you have bad people in the country?'

'So I am told.'

'Lots of bad people where I live. We are not allowed to speak to them. They hang around.'

'Nobody hangs around where I live. It's the bridge, you see. It's hallowed ground.'

'What do you mean, hallowed?'

'Holy.'

'Like a church?'

'Yes. The angels visit. So it must be.'

'You have your own angels!'

'Yes. They are white, have wings and are very beautiful.'

'Gosh.'

Rhys was distinguished because of his good looks. But he was one of those boys who would question, if uncertain. He had a thirst for everyday knowledge, what made things work—the moon, gravity, tides. Wheels, magnifying glasses, street lights. And the sun, the earth and what time do they have breakfast in Australia! He was uncertain about angels, now she had mentioned them.

He gazed at Gabriella. It was unlikely he had considered this before, this thing about girls. It puzzled him. They were different. They accepted stuff, which he would question. And there was this other thing, this association with angels. He had had a mental picture of an angel—its human likeness, its goodness, its serenity. And as he gazed he believed he recognised these qualities in Gabriella.

'You are beautiful,' he said unabashed.

'I don't think so. Just normal.'

'You could be an angel,' said Rhys.

'I don't have wings. Angels must have wings.'

'Why?'

'To fly ... to fly from heaven.' That seemed to satisfy Rhys for a moment before doubt spread across his face. Gabriella, sweetly, gave him a hug. 'And I don't have a long neck!' she added. Now this piece of information taxed Rhys. He wormed free from Gabriella's arms, stood back a little, and examined her carefully before giving his judgement.

'Your neck is a bit short. I'm glad. If you were an angel you would have to be good all the time.'

'Oh, I am good all the time. Where I live, by the bridge, it would be hard to be naughty.'

'I think I would like to live in the country.'

'Let's ask Nannan then.'

And they did.

*

And so it was from then on Rhys spent his holidays at the

cottage in the shadow of the bridge—and for those times orphanhood became the greatest pleasure. The swans remained beautiful, but lost their angelic approbation. With adolescence came the acceptance of reality, sad though this was. Through all the seasons Nannan watched them play as she had watched her Bleddyn and Liliwen play. In the snow in the winter, and in the water by the bridge in the summer. Huddled in clothes. Or naked with white, developing bodies, until age constrained. Alarmingly, Nannan sensed inevitability, a foreboding.

In their twelfth year Rhys carved their initials.

Nannan watched him from the windows of the cottage as she had watched her Bleddyn. Chisel in hand, and with care the letters R and G were nitched into the opposite midway timber of the bridge.

Nannan took them once a week to the swimming baths in the town for swimming lessons. Although they could swim she wanted them to be not only good swimmers and strong swimmers, but lifesavers as well. In their own way they were beautiful. They could not avoid it. Wingless, neckless otherwise like the swans. Humans who learned to hiss and snort and grunt like the swans. Neither was distinguished either by sin or by virtue. Inseparable, one seldom being seen without the other. They swam and frolicked with the swans in the waters beneath the bridge. They played this game. When either shouted '*Inca*' they had to jump from the bridge into the water below. They never married, but were as close as any two could be. Nannan passed away, and Rhys moved into the cottage. He was there during the great flood that washed away the bridge and sent the swans into exile. He built a replacement bridge in the fashion of a traditional Inca suspension bridge made from grass and woven by hand. It was called Pepita's Bridge.

It carried visitors and curious ramblers the short distance in single file, and became synonymous with the care line Gabriella and Rhys established to help orphans in spiritual need. Orphans came, stayed in the cottage for a while, rested, and were emboldened with hope and love. The swans returned, and built their nest from the same long grasses from which Rhys had woven to make the bridge.

Pieces of wood from the old bridge were found down stream. The midway timbers into which the two sets of initials had been carved were recovered. These became part of the uprights that carried the message to the unpossessed.

Life is a bridge—it carries love.

A Bungalow in Keston

'Hallelujah.' I think not … not any more!

*

Am I expected to express joy at the flowers—the ritual birthday present? It is hard to feel grateful. The hollowness of it while they continue to sweep under the carpet what I wish for. Why do they not listen, sense my pain beneath the clouds of their onslaught—and yes, their bigotry? They do not listen. Just give me a breath of kindness, a touch of compassion, not another bunch of sugar-encrusted aromas to insensitive the hurt. I remember the togetherness we once celebrated in Bromley: those collaborative birthdays where happiness represented aspiring lives—before charity became humbled by controversy.

Where is the gain from their covetous, grinding pursuit of the benefits of my twilight?

*

I feel history in my bungalow, and I share the ghosts of peoples' past who once lived within its walls. It was built after WW1 in rural Keston (as it was then) beyond the London conurbation of Bromley. Built by a returning manager of a colonial tea plantation in West Bengal—the replica of his bungalow in India. Thus, it was out of character amidst the other dwellings at the time, and those others more lately built when the tides of suburbia rose through necessity. Its façade faces the road along those newer tides that now penetrate twice a day. The rush-hour tides of traffic in the morning and again in the evening. It's a tidal sort of place, really, where feelings rise and fall with every headline, with every garden fence dispute, with every rowdy neighbour, with every rowdy neighbour's dog—within the intricacies of a close-knit community, where courtesies sometimes play second fiddle to money. Oh yes! The bourgeoisie reign supreme, and the older generation who rest behind lace curtains and are not inclined to rock the boat whatever the tide!

Few now climb the wooden steps to my verandah and enter the front door. Those that do glance at the hidden treasures that age has bestowed on me. I notice the raised eyebrows, which are not raised in contempt for only do I see eyes that acquaint antiquity with farewell sadness and the generational dust with infirmity. My life savings have been spent obtaining Indian artefacts, which I believe to be relevant. I have never been to India, but have observed with delight the majesty, the artistry of so much that is Indian. I just love my Indian carpets that cover my floorboards. I can smell India every time I walk on them as the dust rises. Oh! I never Hoover them. I love the dust—too precious to bin. And they have aged as I have become too fragile for powerful suction!

Bangla, very Indian, is the name of my bungalow. It has

been called that since the retired tea planter had it built. I am pleased no occupant has wished to change it. Sometimes I put on a sari and cook a curry. Then I sit and dream. These are the times I hope never to forget. I regurgitate them for fear of this—the day I bought the bungalow, my father's birthday, the passing of my mother, the day they carved my best beloved's name on Portland stone. My husband, then. Forever I would have led a life of mediocrity had it not been for those with whom I shared my younger days. And the two children I fostered. I remember their birthdays, the fun days out with them. Their tears and laughter. Their perky wide-eyed faces—and the day they left. Almost adult they were then. That was before I moved into Bangla, long before the day the Indian gentleman came. This I cannot forget. Up the wooden steps he came, unannounced, courteously and called me *memsahib*. Certainly past my prime then, but on he came, graciously, such fine manners not often found in Western gentlemen. Just passing, he said. Did not wish to disturb me. Could not but wonder at my little bit of India, my Bangla in Keston, and to meet its resident. I just have to tell you, dear Reader, it was he who bought me my first sari. I wept, it was beautiful. I wept because no man had ever bought me a dress. I still weep when I remember these things, these times. Those halcyon days when time was worshiped and God protected.

Such a dapper-dressed man he was! Indeed, straightway I noticed he was dressed much in the style I imagined worn by the colonial masters beneath whom his forefathers would have lived. Collar and tie, tightish trousers, tailored jacket and finely polished shoes. He carried a Malacca walking cane with just that touch of swagger ennobled by the gentry. He wore a plain Fedora hat, which he first raised from politeness and then removed as he crossed the threshold of the bungalow. All this I noticed, and remember clearly. And his tie with an avian motif spread at regular intervals proudly suggestive of an association. Later he told me the bird was a Baya weaver common in West Bengal. For a while he just stood and stared, overwhelmed at the furnishing of the room, and marveling at this fragment of big India in little Keston, south London.

'May I?' he asked stepping further into the room. 'I can tell you have Indian connections. Indeed, yes ...'

I interrupted. '... Only since I was fortunate to buy this bungalow. From then on India became my second home, as it were. If I were granted my roots again surely I would choose India ... and become Indian.'

'Ah ... then we may have passed in the Indian Ocean!' He smiled. I am second generation Indian living here. My father was employed on the Underground.'

'And you?' I asked.

'Oh, no! I worked in textiles.'

I could tell he was contented with that. Wishing him not to hurry away I offered him a cup of tea.

'That would be most kind.'

I showed him to the rattan chair—the comfy one with cushions, took his hat and cane and stowed them in a corner.

'Shan't be a moment,' I said. 'Masala chai? I have some prepared.'

'Oh, yes indeed ... most kind.'

I arranged the tea on my woven-patterned tray. I reached up in the cupboard for the Royal Crown Derby Blue Mikado cups and saucers (which I bring out on special occasions) and were prized by my parents. And, as if owing allegiance to Keston, I opened a packet of digestive biscuits. These I distributed on a plebian plate barren of artistry.

So there we sat, and dawn's twilight slowly rose.

*

He was a man difficult to age. I put him to be over seventy. Physically well able and worldly reserved. He lived the other side of the common, at Hayes, and said he often walked across the common for exercise. When I brought in the tea he stood up and stretched out his hand.

'Bipin,' he said. 'Bipin Buburam.'

'Gloria,' I said, and shook his hand.

The conversation went with refreshing ease.

When he left that day I was emboldened to say I hoped he would call again.

'*Bidaya*,' he said. His face expressed pleasure.

Many weeks passed before he called a second time.

*

Then, unannounced, I heard his footfalls and the taps of his cane on the wooden steps. Unhurried they were, yet with the sense of purpose. Steadily they came, with confidence. I liked that. I knew it was he, before I opened the door. It was as if he knew he would be welcome.

*

I reflect frequently. Of late I gaze at my mirror image and talk to myself. My face has changed. Its lines are less obvious—or am I deceiving myself? I am confronted by a problem, dear Reader; should consciousness continue to extend unselfish consideration toward my foster children? Only did I foster these two, and for both of them the years of harbouring were their critical years—the decade between the ages of six and sixteen. First Paul, then Sophia. Contented years they were. A happy family, we were: well integrated, friendly yet keeping our own counsel. The other side of Bromley we lived then. It was not until they left home I moved into Bangla. They went their ways and I mine. It was a parting, but at the time with no sense of perpetuity. Yet Bangla and the Indian gentleman freaked them out. So I talk to my face as if my face belonged to another, a stranger and I say: Surely anomalous must have a bearing on their subsequent attitude, this sudden deviation from the expected—their debasement of all things Indian, which was quite sudden.

Paul and Sophie were as one. That is they became inseparable. It had been lovely to watch them grow up together, and my friends were complementary about their closeness and how they looked after each other. Their affection was openly visible, and a joy to witness. They shared their sweets, their breakfast toast, their pens, paper and school homework. If they had come from separate families I would have, eventually, worried their intimacy was too concentrated. They would walk arm-in-arm, their school satchels swinging in unison—happily. However, when they were fourteen I received a letter from their school. It was courteous, from the headmistress, some of it about their academic progress, but a section was personal (I considered from the borders of a headmistress's remit). This troubled me.

... I have observed the closeness Paul and Sophie have for each other, and the small variations in their academic work. I am concerned that amongst their peers they are isolating themselves. I often see them during breaks huddled together in singular communion. This may be a passing phase. They need to mingle more and learn the benefits of integration.

I thought them happy, contented and loving children: that the mutual empathy they possessed did not affect these characteristics. Rather, I saw it as enhancing them. Nevertheless, I gave the headmistress's comments due regard and wrote a note thanking her for drawing my attention to it. As children did they have a sense of their earlier dispersion— and subsequently a gradual unifying coming together?

They were sharp kids, and about them hung something of a survivors' mentality. Not overconfident, but quietly in front of the curve for their ages on many matters. I believe they came to learn the home I had provided for them was their home, and that they belonged there by some inherent right. Yet, having received the headmistress's letter my views altered and I began to see in Paul and Sophie a conspiracy, a plan to counter any changes in their circumstances because they understood they were vulnerable and not quite as permanent as they had grown to believe.

*

Paul and Sophie went happily to university. As orphaned, as it were, by their biological mothers yet remaining tethered loosely to a fostering mother. My man had long gone—taken from me by war. And the biological fathers of my two foster children had also turned out to be transient leaving both mothers unable to cope. Paul and Sophie had not chanced to learn the function of fatherhood, indeed in hindsight I think they may well have considered all fathers irrelevant, an unnecessary addition within the structure of life.

*

Dapper. Alert. There stood Bipin on my threshold. Lovely Indian smile. Genuine. Opened his arms, a little way. Such a gentleman!

'Good morning, Gloria. It would be wrong for me to say I was just passing. Why, such a bright day I said to myself, I'll cross the common and see if Gloria is in.'

'Well, I am,' I said, perhaps a bit too gleefully.

So in he came. I sat him in the rattan chair and placed his Malacca walking cane in the corner.

'Masala chai?' So easy, I thought, with this gentleman. Quite homely.

'That would be nice … goes well with a walk in the common.'

Different tie, I noticed. Saffron, and perfectly tied.

Out came the Crown Derby.

No digestive biscuits—empty tin!

Why did I think the conversation that was to follow significant? It was probably the ease with which it was conducted. The free flow of the listened words. The smiles, too, mingling with harmonious chuckles! There was a discovery: this discovery not through a sense of purpose, but by the essential nature of shared idiosyncrasies. He was modest—I had the feeling he underplayed his hand because he believed his abilities were less important than the manner in which he had employed them. Between us I perceived gifted and gentle naturalness that extended throughout the rhythmic breathing of cordial conversation.

'You live alone. No children?' Bipin began when he had settled.

'Just the two ... both fostered. Then it was uni for them. They sort of vanished. Took up their own lives. They were grateful I had provided a safe home for them, I could tell. But then their silence, the conditional abandonment I found difficult to adjust to. The sudden emptiness from youthful gaiety and ambition—and yes, their appreciation. I loved that. But life fell silent when they left. So I bought Bangla, fabricated a new life, as it were, licked my wounds of abandonment and refreshed my soul. Became *Indian* ... and stretched out for compassion with a desire to give it. I ceased to take on the smaller wrongs of life, became submissive, yet the desire to think only of myself thwarted the needs of compassion and distracted myself from the real world'.

Bipin raised his eyebrows, so I put on a brighter expression. And with the touch of light banter I added: 'To walk across the common to see a single lady would suggest you also live alone.' An appreciative smile then, and with a twinkle of the eye he responded:

'Ah! Yes. A lady in an Indian house with English discernment ... we have shared this planet.'

'I am seventy-nine years old.' Why did I suddenly say

that! 'There we are then! And I, well ... no more than two years ahead of you!'

We talked about the weather then—very English! And he about his treasured 1954 Morris Minor. A classic beauty. Restored. Colour important, he said. Green for rebirth, and envy too. And your wife? I asked. A bit bold for me not knowing if he ever had one: but that is how it was, this ability to flow the conversation without fear of impropriety.

'My beautiful wife, Charu.' Deep in thought then. Just for a while.

'Tell me about her,' I asked. 'Only if you would like to.'

'It is a life to tell.' Bipin's eyes focused on his teacup until he found the requisite words. 'She was second generation, like myself. Born in Sydenham ... but deep down very much a heritage Indian. Western clothes ... no problem. Saris always her favourite. Looked beautiful whatever. Indeed, yes, I found her amongst the cottons! ... in the textile business where I had been taken on.' He smiled benevolently as he recollected the moment. 'Always surrounded by a mass of colours she was ... processing orders, getting the colour mixes correct. I thought very responsible when I first saw her working. Her eyes cast sown, confident. Modest ... oh yes, so modest, but later I pondered if there was a touch of coquetry ... that feminine charm that can be both lovely and lethal. It did not take me long for me to realize she was empowered by modesty ... that ethereal quality that sits generously on the shoulders of many Indian ladies. That first day, day one of my ignited life, I was just a trainee manager. She never looked up. Thereafter, I became a visitor whenever I could, to the lines she was supervising. We bore no children. Indeed, I believe that to be the only sadness during our long and congenial marriage. We married, we worked together, we rose up together through the ranks of the business and we retired together. Then, one day not many years ago now, she said she felt unwell and passed peacefully away without fuss … and little warning. So like her, just so like her.' Bipin sipped his tea. I could tell his eyes had filled with tears. I gave him time. Then he looked at me, straight. 'We were beautiful together,' he said. The way he said it struck me. Yes, his accent was delicate, but it was his eyes—the depth of their sadness overwhelming his thoughts. I had a feeling then, and still do, of a man once engulfed by grief whilst the wake of his beautiful life partner continued to stretch like a ship's towards the horizon. Then curiously he brightened. 'Loneliness is a pandemic … there is too much of it about. Life does go on, and companionship a palliative.'

'The young have no reason to understand, do they?' They become suspicious when the old begin a new relationship. They worry the assets that should fall to them via natural inheritance may be syphoned off as well as the love engendered over time. The speed with which loneliness can descend can disorientate and wobble feelings that have rested secured for decades.'

'Yes, that is quite so.'

'For me, when my fostered children left home, a quietness first engulfed me, then a foreboding sense of abandonment took over. It was the offering for sale of the bungalow that inspired me to begin a different life. So I bought it as a no-going-back stepping-stone to personal reformation.'

'Ah! ... You are stronger than I. I have floundered unable to come to terms with fate.'

'Perhaps you have indulged in self-pity, which is the prerogative of grief.'

*

It was after Bipin's second visit I became aware of the advancing disagreement from Paul and Sophia. The suggestion I was too enthusiastic about Bipin's attributes. They never did call him Bipin—it was always *the Indian* as if they saw him as no other than a pampered being to his own well-being, some kind of upstart on the make. The first time they came face-to-face with him their rudeness was an embarrassment and hurtful. When they next visited I said: One thing university has not taught you is good manners, and your personal opinions should not be at the expense of courtesy and never at the expense of your mother or in your own home. They took great offence at that! You are not our mother and this is not our home, they spat out. It was true, of course. Their biological mothers were somewhere, and their home had never been the bungalow but a house the other side of Bromley.

In fairness to them they never forget to send flowers on my birthday.

But it was understanding I needed.

*

What finally drove them away?

The sari. The one my beloved Bipin had given me. They arrived one afternoon without warning many months after

Bipin passed away. They may have come with good intentions, but if they had these were cast aside when they saw me dressed in the sari. It is peacock blue with embroidered gold trim: simple but stunning. Having shown me how to wear it Bipin said I looked like a true Indian woman, and just as elegant. For special occasions, he had added. I only ever wore it when I was with him—either in Bangla or when we went out together. The day my foster children appeared I was wearing it in quiet remembrance of Bipin's birthday. He would have been eighty-five. I know he would have appreciated the gesture. Well, it was more than a gesture: it was like a thanksgiving for his kindness to me, and his spiritual generosity—a celebration in his absence.

Well, Paul and Sophia ruined that!—imperiously denouncing by insinuation my wisdom and perspective.

I shall forever remember the tremor created during their acrimonious departure as their footfalls descended Bangla's wooden steps. I learnt, that pivotal afternoon, how much emotional atmosphere of a place can be interpreted from departing feet, just as I had come to understand arriving soles, which carry love and empathy. Paul and Sophie left the door open during their rapid exit. I stood in the full bloom of blue and gold while drowning in the ashes of family harmony. I tried to wave farewell, perhaps to cling on to a vestige of kinship. They did not look back as if neither I nor my home were worth a second glance.

*

When they had gone I sat back and stared at the empty rattan chair, which was Bipin's chair. I let the tears roll down my cheeks, like blood-letting, the panacea for distress. The overwhelming realization of emptiness and deprivation, my erasure from the lives of Paul and Sophia whom I had loved with generosity, but whose feelings I must have misunderstood and of whom I cannot have thought deeply enough. Biological kinship; that irreplaceable bond of blood inherently absent in the fostering process weighed heavily on me.

I asked myself: Had it been self-interest that I had bought the bungalow? And had it been self-interest that I had emboldened Bipin?

Sadly, it could be arguably so. I remember their words as I sit and dream:

This Indian fantasy is no more than a pretentious panto-mime. Look at you! Dressed in a make-believe costume like a theatrical dame with some foppish gentleman bedecked like a colonial administrator. Slapstick! Surprised you are not strumming a sitar! You are not the mother we knew, and this bungalow is not the home we knew. Mother, you are a Londoner not a Bengali!

This they had thrown at me, just before they left, and I stepped in telling them they were right. He is a gentleman who turns himself out with a sense of pride. He is a kindly soul, and that I was sorry it offended them to have a mother who has found companionship a comfort in her twilight years. You have your life ahead of you and one day you will grow old, then you will discover the mistaken moments during your maturing years. I have always done my best for you. I need no more in return save respect, which implies consideration for the aging process.

Consumed by hostility, they were. Just the flowers on my birthday, now. I know I should be grateful for that.

*

Bipin will not come back. He is with his Charu. I pray time will give me a chance to see my children again. I have aged since Bipin passed away. Hurt has no cure other than reconciliation. Only silence is left. But my evening years with Bipin were a gift from God. His Malacca cane stands witness in its corner. It is his presence. Each day I brush it with my hand.

Some day now, quite soon, I shall need it to steady myself as I go up and down my wooden steps.

The Veteran and the Italian Girl

Without doubt it was a cottage. It spoilt no one's view. It had picket fencing on its lane side, and the original hazel arch had rotted into obscurity. For a generation Nature had grasped the cottage freehold and laid upon it the foundations of dereliction and beauty. It was where the veteran lived, where his father had taken root after returning from the Italian campaign. From young boy to manhood the veteran had been raised there—this cottage, this lane, beneath a long-gone arch he would have ventured into a world where Nature would sow the seeds of carelessness into his inner self. The cottage was without neighbours, a lonely vista on the periphery of the village. On each side rested narrow strips of abandoned farmland now home to patches of bracken, grassed-over molehills and neglected rabbit warrens. Hemmed in, as it were, seemingly without love. Yet its name suggested otherwise. Lettered in black on a piece of white board the name of the cottage had abided time to hold its clarity. *Agro Pontino* it declared. And elsewhere, in the wood store at the back an earlier version, discarded— *Pontine Fields*. Both had been crudely written by the veteran's father, the drips and trickles of black paint still visible. He had returned to his disillusioned wife who soon decamped to dissimilar pastures.

She left behind a son for a faltering father to raise.

This son, christened Jim but commonly to become known in the village as 'the veteran' for he had followed in his father's footsteps and enlisted in the local infantry regiment. In a jocular manner the moniker 'Jumbo' had been given to him by his comrades-in-arms because he was a burley, well-built man of great strength. He had, after many years of service, been discharged on medical grounds because he had contracted bilharzia whilst serving in Africa. Apart from the physical discomforts from the disease his mental faculties were affected. His moniker continued to be used in the village after his discharge, but with less waggish significance that unpleasantly evoked the burly, the ugly, the menacing—a dangerous man not to be crossed on a dark night. In time he became as lonely as his cottage, and as disregarded by human empathy as the little acreage of his garden. He looked out on no fervent pastures, companionship evaded him. His father, on whom he relied, passed away, the years slid by, the village torments lost their sting, age encroached his whole self, allowing sterility to take control. Unseen he faded whilst his cottage garden flourished according to the seasons. Blooms opened to fragrance and brightness—to palettes of colour, which did not mirror its hueless resident.

*

One spring day when the weather was at peace and about the cottage hung the accustomed ennui a circumstance befell the veteran. He had a visitor. The cottage and its garden resting unattended awaited no such occasion. The wicket gate, hitched upon rusted hinges, from which the name *Agro Portino*, hung precariously. Close by, and part buried by euphobia, an old bread bin squatted for the benefit of the postman. Ivy trailed up the posts of the gate. An original brick path, herringbone in design, led directly to the door of the cottage. No edges of the path were visible, encircled as they were by riots of self-seeded lilies of the valley, forget-me-nots—and the early signs of cow parsley spreading from beneath a crab apple tree. Of the cottage not much was visible from the lane screened off, as it were, by Nature's abundance. The front door was painted brown, sash windows on either side, a water butt stood beneath a drainpipe, some old wooden vegetable boxes lay higgledy-piggledy under the windows. A saucepan and a wooden spoon hung from a bracket should any caller seek attention. The cottage's façade, whose brickwork suggested endurance, was part covered by an old climbing rose. Its spring bloom had for as long as any could remember produced a deep pink majestic blush, which gave the hallmark of love and permanency. Behind the cottage overshadowing the wood store stood, now laden with blossom, an apple tree of considerable age and a quince tree. The front garden, this spring, had had profusions of daffodils, tulips and hyacinths all competing for space. Lilac and choisya and weigela weighed in offering paintbox pastels of pinks and whites and pale purples. The red-barked cornus grew sternly erect beside an exochorda amidst a riot of unhurried flora whose tapestry of rich colours proved an ability to apportion without the help of Man.

No sign of the veteran disturbed the natural enrichment: no eyes could pass this place without a second glance: no sound penetrated the bucolic air—and no place in the world could emulate the penetrative silence of this English scene.

*

A bird with an eye of an eagle would have spotted the distant speck—the cyclist with its fluttering flag. It was propelled with rhythmic purpose and gritty determination, its wheels as far as the eyes could tell, making slow and little distance. The lane meandered here and there, and sight of the bicycle was occasionally lost as it passed beneath trees and negotiated concealed curves. From his cottage window the veteran, too, had spotted the bicycle and he had begun to follow its now obvious progress along the lane with a sharpening interest. As it came closer the fluttering flag evoked supremacy, was emblematic, which disquieted him. Nevertheless, he continued to watch its progress attaching fearful purpose to the red-painted metalwork of the bicycle and the arrogant size of the flag. Closer on it came until he saw its helmeted rider resolutely intent on progress. Behind the foliage of his front garden the bicycle suddenly slowed before coming to a rest at the wicket gate. The flag, losing momentum, drooped.

The cyclist, a young woman, took off her helmet and shook out her hair. She took a photograph of the gate. The veteran peered, watched with concentrated eye. She propped the bicycle against the picket fence, and studied the path to the front door before carefully opening the gate lest it fell away from its moorings. Up the path she strode confidence prevailing over ambivalence. The veteran moved back from the window, vanished into the shadows. The cyclist studied the saucepan and wooden spoon, worked out its usage and gave it a hearty bang. The veteran wished her away. To him she appeared a harbinger of trouble, her bicycle a flash of dangerous red. And the boldness of her!—like the village people who once mocked him, who had erased all his confidence, who had driven him into squalid isolation. He calculated this caller was one of those. She banged a second time with more vigour than the first. She stood back from the cottage taking in the whole, sensed, a sound maybe, that someone was at home.

'Ciao,' she called out. 'Ciao'.

A worn path led around the back. She followed it, called out 'ciao' again at the back door and getting no response she was minded to return to her bicycle and continue her journey. At the front she was surprised to find the cottage door open and a heavily built man filling its frame. Without expression or emotion he stood in silence, eyeing her. Not unfriendly, just vacant. His trousers held up by braces over a dirty white vest. Just socks, no shoes, stubbled chin, balding, There was much of him to suggest he had not long stirred himself and had no expectation of a purposeful day.

'Ciao ... Hello,' she said. 'Parli italiano?' The veteran remained motionless like a statue made from granite—without expression. 'Agro Portino!' She pointed to the gate. 'Are you Italian, parli italiano?' She shrugged her shoulders, threw wide her arms, palms uppermost in mild desperation, and breaking into passable English added: 'I am Italian.

You have garden with colour. Very English! Agro Portino ... Portino Fields. I know area.' The manner, her accent and the words 'Portino Fields' had an effect on the veteran. He moved: not much, but he moved. His eyelids fluttered and his eyes became cautiously receptive. They sought some kind of clarity, some focus. He held his ground. Silence, through which thoughts travelled in both directions. Then the veteran slowly opened his mouth and spoke softly for a big man.

'My father ... he's been there.'

That could have been the end of the conversation, but he added after a pause

'In the war.'

The lady, sensing a more helpful attitude, more approachable, responded in a bright and relaxed demeanour.

'I am Mirabella from Italy. They call me Bella.'

The veteran, although detecting the brush of genuine warmth, did not step forward in polite greeting. His face contorted a weak grimace, which in fairness to him was an underused beam long unaccustomed.

*

There was something independent about Bella. Not that she had, presumably, cycled across Europe on her own, but her manner broadcast a confidence and from her face shone rude health and worldly sparkle. Nevertheless, to the veteran's failing brain the whole Bella appeared an embodiment of a traveller going places—and with a flag to claim a place! He would never be able to articulate this thought accepting her only as 'foreign'. But he did feel at ease, safe on his own patch, which was a feeling he had not felt since his father had passed away. He relaxed. And so it was the built-up tension brought on by her arrival slipped away in appraisal of a friendly encounter.

'Belissimo giardino', she gesticulated waiving her arms. 'Tazza di te,' she joked. The veteran stepped forward, beamed again. Bella noticed his arms lacked control; they dangled, and were mottled with rash. He was unsteady, a pitiful sight for a big man, any man. A man surely overtaken by circumstance. Yet his garden flourished. 'Bellissimo fiori' she said. He beamed again. He was making an effort. Beyond the open door Bella could see signs of a home prevailing amidst neglect. Rubbish littered the floor, a chair without its seat, a table with unwashed crockery. Behind the cottage there was a wooden bench with its back beneath the apple tree. It was lichen-stained, and the grass on which it stood was trampled flat exposing patches of dry earth. 'La panca ... bench. I sit there. Rest.' The veteran followed her. She sat down, stretched her legs and gave a long sigh of comfort—closed her eyes for a few seconds. The veteran stared down at her, and signs of genuine awareness spread amongst the wrinkles of his face. 'Tazza di te,' she said dreamingly, then without further ado collected herself and went to get her brewing kit from her bicycle. The veteran began to follow her, changed his mind and returned to stand by the bench.

Language played a part, yet from the few words that were spoken a grasp of intention was gathered by eyes and expressions. Only after Bella had set up her small heater and unwrapped a square of hexamine did the veteran brighten. From the outside tap she filled a little kettle and placed a camper's mug on the bench beside her.

In all matters outwardly present the veteran and Bella had nothing in common. Age divided them. The veteran stagnant: Bella flowing. She had an alert brain, he did not. They faced each other in a place where neglect and beauty rested in harmony. The solitary quiet was fragile and sympathetic, submerged there lurked a sparkle—the trip of fellow-feeling, the breath of inclusion. Bella was touched by the pitiful sight of the man before her. She muttered in Italian as she made the tea. The veteran stood looking down on her, her seated figure: upon his face now a permanent beam. He was amused to see a foreign person brewing tea in his garden. Not just an ordinary brew, but one using a hexamine tablet similar to those familiar in the army. Its distinctive smell conjuring again fragments of a life once led. Bella tapped her mug, stretched it out towards the veteran, brought it to her lips.

'Mug. You have mug, I make you tea.'

The veteran understood.

This simple act of a very British tradition let contentment to settle and smother any suggestion of disquiet. A grubby mug was found, tea was drunk without conversation, an understanding made present.

'Il tuo campo ... your field?' Bella pointed over the boundary of the garden. The veteran nodded, which gave no clue as to whether he understood. 'Piantare una tenda ... pitch tent in field.' She described by waving her arms the outline of a tent and the banging in of the pegs. The veteran found this amusing and gave forth a throaty laugh nodding his head quite violently at the same time. That seemingly being agreed upon Bella stretched her legs by walking around the garden, and the veteran following like a shadow his empty mug dangling from his little finger.

*

So, dear Reader, up went her tent and her bicycle propped inside the boundary fence. Tidy she was. Experienced camper. Sorted before the sun went down. And as if to stake her claims she fixed firmly the Italian flag into the ground. Flutter it did in the most gentle of breezes. Satisfied with her space she went back to the cottage and gave the saucepan a hearty bang. The door was opened immediately. There stood the veteran, big beam, almost expectant.

'I cook supper for you … Ti cucino la campo … in field.'

*

She laid out a plastic sheet. He brought over the garden bench. On the sheet Bella had placed the ingredients—spaghetti, butter, grated Parmesan cheese, herbs. A couple of camping plates, the cooker, the hexamine, a wooden spoon and two disposable forks. The veteran stood gazing at the purposeful arrangement until, at long last, he sat down on the bench an achievement that gave her kindly disposition a fillip to see him warming to her, to trusting her. Sitting, perhaps at peace with his inner self.

She boiled the water and slipped in the spaghetti. The veteran watched keenly the subsequent draining and the adding of each ingredient—and finally the tossing of the pasta meal. He beamed. He nodded. Just the two of them, this spring evening—this dilapidated giant and this Italian adventuress beneath a declining sun. And across the fence the cottage garden slumbered. Bella was aware she was reducing by degrees the giant's burden like a therapist administrating transitory succour to an inflicted man.

They ate. The flag fluttered gently reminding not all was this an English countryside with its pastures symbolic of a green and pleasant land, but humbly the aroma from the Italian meal and the sentiment of Pontine Fields.

'Il Tricolore,' said Bella pointing to the flag.

The veteran tried to repeat this, stumbled, fell silent.

'Il Tricolore,' she said more slowly.

The veteran tried again. This time with success—he chortled.

They both smiled: with generosity they looked at each other. The pleasantness of achievement spread widely over their faces.

'Verde, bianca, rossa,' said Bella pointing towards the flag. 'The colours ... hope, faith, charity,' she added.

*

The following morning from his cottage window the veteran saw the flag limply aloft. Of Bella, her tent and her red-painted bicycle there was no sign. Only the flag remained abandoned and solitary.

'Life?' questioned the veteran melancholically before turning away to face another day.

www.ingramcontent.com/pod-product-compliance
Lightning Source LLC
Chambersburg PA
CBHW051849170626
46807CB00003B/1398